My Café Cubano

To Frank —
Thank you
for your support!
All the best,

6/21/14

My
CAFÉ CUBANO

A story of loss and suffering under Fidel Castro's regime

A NOVEL BY

CRISTINA GRACIELA

ORIENTE
HOUSE

Published 2007 by Oriente House in the United States of America.

FIRST EDITION

Library of Congress Control Number: 2007925707

ISBN 978-0-9794877-0-5

For Buelo

Author's Note

There is much truth in the following account. However, the book is a work of fiction based on my family's experiences during and immediately following the Cuban Revolution at the end of the 1950s. Names, dates and ages have been changed for privacy.

Fidel Castro began as a guerilla leader in the Sierra Maestra, a mountain range located in the southernmost province of Cuba. From his mountain camp he systematically attacked and eventually overthrew the corrupt dictatorship of Fulgencio Batista on January 1, 1959. At the base of the Sierra Maestra lies a small, prosperous town, Bayamo, where my mother was born and raised until Castro's conquest of Cuba signaled the end of a way of life for the small island nation. By 1961, a mass exodus of people started to make their way primarily to the United States.

References to historical events and names are used throughout the novel, but the characters are fictitious. Any reference to actual persons is purely coincidence. This is my family's story in my own words.

Introduction

by Isabela Daniela de Leon

My grandfather owned the Cuban version of Starbucks®
until Castro confiscated all of his property in 1961 and
declared a state of socialism. It would take *El Monstruo* (The
Monster) more than one year to openly declare himself a
communist. My family was long gone by then, leaving
behind a chain of cafés from coast to coast and city to city.

The children, including my mother, were sent out of
the country first, not by choice, and picked up in Miami,
Florida by various relatives including cousins and an aunt
and uncle. Because of my grandfather's businesses, vast
holdings, wealth and social standing, my grandparents were
forced to stay behind and assume false identities, rent a
place on the beach and wait three agonizingly long months
to join their children in America. Using false papers and
over $10,000 in *mordida* (bribe money), they paid off a
communist official and obtained flights out of Havana on
New Year's Day of 1962 – one of the happiest and saddest
days of their lives.

They arrived in Miami poor – essentially flat broke –
with little knowledge of the English language and in a
strange land. America welcomed them with open arms
under the political asylum policy established for Cuban
refugees. Like the majority of the Cubans that came to this
country in the early 1960s, they quickly reestablished
themselves and rebuilt their lives.

I heard countless stories in my youth, a living oral
history of the sights, sounds and smells of Cuba. For all of
the terror they endured, I heard love and longing emerge as
their stories unfolded.

I longed to see Cuba first hand, but *El Monstruo* simply would not die! When would my chance come to visit the land and stories of my childhood? My family, unlike other Cuban exiles, was not fooled by Castro. Many exiles left their homeland thinking it was a temporary arrangement – the revolution would die, the government would be overthrown, they would outlive Castro. Yet, Castro lived through fabled CIA assassination attempts. He managed to hold the country together after Russian aid ended in the 1990s along with the end of the Cold War. Castro was pushing 70 and still strong as ever.

My parents felt betrayed when I announced my intentions of visiting Cuba as a college graduation present to myself. I was almost 22 and impatient to see things. How could I visit a communist nation? How could I go travel there while Castro was still in power? Why would I endanger myself and their hopes for my freedom? I couldn't answer all of these questions, but I felt compelled to visit.

My cousin, Manny, had already booked a flight to Havana scheduled to leave three weeks after graduation to visit his ailing grandmother. She had little time now and was at a rest home in Bayamo, my mother's hometown. Manny, ten years my elder and male, would be an excellent chaperone. The timing was perfect. I would not be deterred and decided to join Manny despite my parents' protests.

Amid tears at the airport my mom confessed to a diary she had begun during the revolution at the age of 14. She wrote in it, on and off, for three years and had hidden the notebooks in a small metal strongbox from my grandfather's home office. She had then hidden the box under a loose panel in her armoire.

I would stay at least one or two nights at her birth home where my grandmother's brother and family resided since my family had fled. My mom said I would have plenty of time to search for the notebooks. She handed me two empty notebooks and begged me to place them in my backpack. I would be searched upon arrival in Havana, and careful inventory of my possessions would take place. Upon exiting Cuba, my bags would be counter checked against the original list. She asked me to switch notebooks, leave the new ones behind and smuggle out her diary.

"Be careful *mi hija*," daughter and "Now you will understand why I didn't want you to visit Cuba until *El Monstruo* was dead," were the last words my mom spoke as I boarded the plane.

The Diary

of

Daniela Isabela Badilla

Notebook 1

*"Yo soy un hombre sincero
De donde crece la palma,
Y antes de morirme quiero
Echar mis versos del alma."*
José Martí

(I am an honest man
From where the palm trees grow,
And before I die I want
To bestow these verses from my soul.)

5 August 1958

Dear Diary,

I never thought I would be one of those "silly" girls that kept a diary. My girl cousins all have diaries full of wishes, love interests and day-to-day events. Now, I feel that if I don't write down my feelings this instant I will die of sadness and grief.

Nando is dead! Shot to death by the Guardia Civil, Batista's men, last night a kilometer from his parent's ranch. My cousin is, no was, only 22 years old and the one son among five children. How can I get used to referring to him as *was*?

He was the workhorse of the family cattle ranch and hopeful of inheriting the business one day. Yesterday morning he had taken two bulls to Papi's cattle ranch for breeding. It was a long day and dusk arrived before the bulls were trailered behind Nando's truck for the short ride home. Tio Miguel, Papi's administrator and Nando's uncle, went along for the ride to visit with his sister, Nando's mom, Dolores.

At the hospital Tio Miguel told Papi they never saw it coming. That one minute they were coasting along enjoying the balmy weather, watching the sunset and laughing, and the next minute the truck was skidding off the road into a ravine. The force of the crash threw Tio Miguel from the truck. His right knee and thigh were covered in blood and Nando was nowhere in sight. He remembers dragging himself toward the truck yelling "Nando! Nando! Are you okay?"

The truck was only three meters away but it felt like a kilometer because of the searing pain in his leg. Eventually he reached Nando whose leg was partially trapped under the truck.

"Nando wake up! You need to help me. Nando! Wake up!" yelled Tio Miguel. Tio Miguel was worried because Nando's stomach and chest were covered in blood.

The humming of a motor began to register in his mind. At first Tio Miguel thought the truck engine was still running and reached up towards the door. As he was reaching a deep, halting voice yelled "Stop! Do not move! Keep your hands where I can see them."

"*Por favor*... help my nephew. His foot is trapped under the truck and he's bleeding badly," begged Tio Miguel. "*Por favor, ayudame.*"

Two men from the Guardia Civil approached the wreck with machine guns pointed. Their jeep's headlights did not cast enough light to see faces, only uniforms. He heard the one on the left demand "Why were you out so late tonight? There is a strict curfew on the roads after sunset!"

Tio Miguel said "My nephew is hurt. I'm not sure why we crashed. Help us." He was losing blood himself and starting to weaken. "I need to get Nando to the hospital."

The men approached, searched the wreckage for weapons and took their wallets. After checking identities they finally radioed for help. Tio Miguel must have passed out because he doesn't remember what happened next, and he woke up in a hospital bed.

Papi was next to him quietly waiting. "Miguel your wife and children are outside waiting. Would you like to see them? May I ask you a few questions?" asked Papi.

"Nando? Where is Nando?" asked Tio Miguel. "His leg was trapped under the truck. The Guardia, they wouldn't help us right away. Nando didn't look so well," said Miguel.

"Miguel, you've been unconscious for a few hours. The doctors removed two bullets from your leg. They think you will walk again with some rehabilitation," said Papi.

"Bullets? Nando was driving and wrecked the truck. I don't understand," said Miguel. "One minute we were laughing... Are you sure?"

"Yes. The Guardia's men brought you in. The official story from the *capitán* is that your truck looked suspicious. You were observed pulling something that resembled weapons on your trailer. It was dark. It was after curfew. His men were following correct procedure – shoot first and ask questions later," said Papi. "It seems that the 'weapons' were no more that bulls with long horns."

"And, Nando?" asked Miguel.

"I'm so sorry." The men looked at each other for awhile before my grandfather proceeded. "Most likely he was dead before the truck drove off the road. The medical examiner said his torso was almost cut completely across the waist by machine gun fire. I pray to God he did not suffer too much," said Papi.

"I never heard or saw a gun. It all happened so fast. I thought I heard the engine backfire. How can this be?" sobbed Miguel.

"Listen, you need to rest. Your family wants to come in for a moment. Miguel, you must be strong for your family," said Papi. "The *capitán* is on my payroll. He has promised to have the report ready tomorrow. What's done is done. His men thought they had come across guerillas transporting weapons up to the Sierra Maestra and acted accordingly. The Guardia will be completely exonerated of this incident, but he expressed his sympathy for the family," said Papi.

"His sympathy! The pigs!" yelled Miguel.

"Miguel, I am so sorry this happened to you. Everyone is devastated about Nando," said Papi.

Miguel was quietly sobbing again.

"I suggest you calm down. I'm going to go down the hall now to get your wife and children," said Papi.

"I need more time," pleaded Miguel.

"They are impatient. You've been unconscious for hours. Calm down. You can do this. They need to see you with their own eyes. To see that you are okay," said Papi. "The next few days will be hard on us all. Get some sleep. I will see you tomorrow."

7 August 1958

Today the local newspaper placed the following obituary for Nando.

> Fernando Joaquin de Marcelo. Born on February 26, 1936. Died on August 5, 1958. Nando, as he was known by his family and friends, graduated with honors from Colegio Divina Pastora in 1955. He is survived by both parents and four sisters. Nando was an avid hunter and fisherman. He showed early promise as a baseball pitcher but sustained a shoulder injury earlier this year in a work related accident. After graduating, Nando had assumed a full time position working on the family ranch as an administrator.
>
> The family is receiving guests at their home until the 9th of August when he will be laid to rest at the family mausoleum in Cementario Elpidio Estrada at noon, Father Francisco de los Reyes presiding.
>
> Nando died of internal bleeding after losing control of his truck and veering off the side

of the road. He was pronounced dead upon arrival
at the Clinica Hirsel. He was deeply loved and will
be sorely missed by his family and friends. His life
had just begun.

8 August 1958

I've been up for twenty four hours straight. We sat all night
with Tio Ricardo, Tia Dolores and the rest of the family. Tio
Miguel was released from the hospital and stayed for much
of the night.

Nando looked so peaceful. Tia Dolores had dressed
him in his finest suit of black gabardine. No scratches or
bruises on his face or hands. It's hard to believe a machine
gun nearly cut his body in two pieces. I wonder if Tia had to
cut his hair. Did she cover any marks on his body with
makeup? How did she decide on clothes? How did she
dress him without weeping? His left hand proudly
displayed the class ring from school. Tia said he had worn
his ring at all times.

Tio Ricardo has shut down. He doesn't say much.
He stares off in the distance for what seems like hours.
Where is the uncle that always had a joke or treat for me?

My cousins are quiet and sad. They cry for awhile.
They bake. They flitter in and out of the living room where
Nando's body is laid out. I join them from time to time in
the kitchen. If one of them laughs, the others are quick to
reproach her. They are really worried about their mother.

Apparently, Tia Dolores passed out cold when she
was given the news. The doctor from down the street,
Doctor Rodrigo, was immediately sent for. After reviving
her with smelling salts he stayed with her through the initial
crying and screaming. He has been great with her.
Checking on her each day. Prescribing sedatives as needed.

I can tell he's worried about her. She gets more nervous each day.

In a few hours we will walk behind a horse and cart as it slowly pulls Nando's body from the ranch to the family plot at the cemetery, an old rancher's tradition. It's a five kilometer walk, and Mami has warned me to wear comfortable shoes.

I must get some sleep now.

10 August 1958

It rained all during the procession and funeral. I overheard Papi tell someone "God is sad today. A grave injustice has happened on our streets."

We walked slowly from the ranch to the cemetery. The walk must have lasted over two hours. My feet are killing me. God, how can I complain about feet when Nando is dead? I am so selfish!

As we walked I would look back from time to time. The procession grew longer and longer and seemed to spread out more than two blocks. Nobody bothered with umbrellas. The slow drizzle was comforting. It never let up once.

Papi looked so handsome. He reminds me of John Wayne – my favorite movie star when I get to go to the town cinema with my friends. He is so tall, so confident. He gives everyone around him strength. Tio Ricardo is still shut down. Papi helped Tia Dolores most of the way to the cemetery. She would lean in from time to time or just stop and shake her head. She set our slow pace. I know she was not eager to arrive. Nobody was.

Father Francisco said a full mass for Nando. We stood in front of the mausoleum for over an hour. Everyone came by and kissed or hugged Tio and Tia. Some kissed the casket. Eventually only twenty or so of the immediate family were left. As the pallbearers picked up the casket and started to move toward the door of the family mausoleum Tia Dolores began to wail.

"How could you do this to me, God?" she screamed at the sky. "Why? No!"

Papi tried to pick her up as she collapsed, but she fought him off. "Leave me! Why? Why? Why?" she said over and over.

Doctor Rodrigo made her swallow something and stayed with her as she slowly calmed down. "Doctor, *ayudame*. Help me. I can't live this way. My son... he was everything to me," she said.

"Dolores you have four daughters to live for. Your oldest gets married soon. They need you," said Doctor Rodrigo.

Tia eventually hugged her knees into her chest and began to rock gently. Papi was able to get her up and put her in the horse drawn cart where the coffin had been. She sat there looking straight ahead with tears streaming down her face.

12 August 1958

I slept most of yesterday. Mami says that it's normal after so much stress. She brought up a new wound today. Just when I thought I couldn't cry anymore. Mami reminded me that Nando was my escort for my debut into society in September. I completely forgot Mami and Papi booked the grand salon at the Club Deportivo for my fifteenth birthday party. All of Papi's business associates are invited. Family is coming in from as far away as La Habana. My dress was ordered last month. Menus and flowers have to be decided. And, now I have no escort!

I want to call the whole thing off. Papi refuses. He says we must go on as if the country is fine, as if the family is fine. He wants to make a statement to the guerillas that walk down our streets, move guns through our town and spy on us. He has paid off Batista's men, Castro's men and the club for my birthday party, and the party will go on!

"What about Nando?" I ask.

Papi says "Nando would have wanted you to celebrate. He was the first to dance at every party. He had a joke for everyone. He would want this."

Papi is probably right, but who will be my escort? I have to practice dances. I kept stepping on Nando's feet during the waltz.

13 August 1958

Papi has a solution. He will ask one of his business partner's sons to be my escort. I'm so embarrassed. But, I'm secretly excited too. I feel guilty thinking about Nando. I hope he asks Señor Federico's son, Adan. Mami knows I have a crush on him. She nicknamed him Fabuloso. He's tall, dark and handsome.

I feel a little better about having this party.

(Later on)

Papi came home from work and said "Adan has agreed to escort you. He will come over tomorrow to work on the dance."

Mami gave me a wink and said "We'll be ready for him at five o'clock. I will call the dance instructor right now to confirm he is available then. Thank you for doing this."

(Much later)

I can't sleep. I'm so nervous. Fabuloso will be here tomorrow! Thank you. Thank you. Thank you.

14 August 1958

It was awful! I can tell Fabuloso resents me and this dance.

My little shit of a brother, Tony, kept peeking in and out of the living room where we were practicing. I could hear his peals of laughter from the hallway, at times from the backyard. Why does he torment me so? It reminds me of when he was 8 and would take the heads off my dolls and pee inside them. Then he would replace the heads. I would either end up covered in urine, or the smell in my bedroom would get awful after a few days.

As he got older the tricks changed. Tony, nobody calls him by his given name Antonio, would sic his dog on me. He would hide small garden snakes in my armoire. And, his tricks didn't stop with me. He was constantly after the staff. The cook would complain to Mami all the time about bags of bugs in the cupboards. The laundry lady would find chewed gum and toilet paper wadded up in the pockets of his pants. He even threatened the cook once with Papi's .38 caliber revolver for not serving him a shaved ice treat. The list went on and on and on…

God, I'm so stressed. Fabuloso barely looked at me. He would only speak when spoken to. *Ay ya yai*! I don't want to write about it anymore. I'm going to tell Mami and Papi I won't do this. It's just too much stress.

16 August 1958

I'm so happy! Fabuloso lived up to his nickname today. He brought me flowers. He kissed me on the cheek twice.

We danced much better today too! The dance instructor says we move like one person. Every time Fabuloso spun me around I felt fabulous – dizzy, breathless, light. Is this love?

Today, I laugh at everything Tony does. He keeps blowing kisses in my direction and making big goofy eyes at me. Let him. I feel glorious. Nothing can ruin my mood.

17 August 1958

I woke up still feeling wonderful. Everyone was home after the funeral, and I had breakfast with the entire family – Papi, Mami, Tony and my older brother Joaquin. After breakfast Papi announced he had some business up in the mountains and asked Joaquin José, J.J., to join him. Mami was shocked!

"How can you take J.J. up to the mountains? *Estas loco?*" said Mami. "He could be hurt, or worse, shot by Castro's men," she yelled.

"I know what I'm doing. It will be a short trip. We'll be back by tonight," said Papi in a calm voice.

Mami ran from the room.

Papi turned to J.J. and asked again, "Would you like to go for a ride up to the farm in the mountains? I want to check on the operations and progress of the crops."

"Yes, Papi," said J.J.

"Listen, I won't think less of you if you stay home today. There is some danger. I pay off Castro's men each month for protection, so we should be okay. But, you never know," said Papi.

J.J. replied, "I want to go. Give me five minutes to get ready."

Papi said, "You can have fifteen. I need to reassure your mother."

I followed J.J. back to his room. Tony followed behind me. I had so many questions. J.J. was in no mood to talk. He promised to fill us in tonight. He practically pushed us out of the room so he could get ready.

Tony and I spent the day with Mami shopping. She wanted to buy us some things for school. We have to go

back in September. Tony and I attend Divina Pastora where
Nando graduated last year. We ordered uniforms at the
seamstress's shop, Tienda Gloria.

Señora Gloria says I have grown over the summer. I
am already over five feet tall. Tony calls me Olive Oyl from
the Popeye cartoons because I am very skinny and bony
looking. He says I have huge eyes and dark hair just like
Popeye's girlfriend.

Tony is tall for his age. He is 12 years old and
almost as tall as I am. He has dark hair too, but his eyes are
green. I wish I had green eyes. J.J.'s eyes are light too. He
got Papi's lighter hair color and is a very dirty blonde. J.J.
attends boarding school in Camaguey. I wonder if Mami
and Papi will send Tony away too. As much as he drives me
crazy, it would be very quiet if both brothers were away
from home.

The three of us had lunch in town. Tony talked
Mami into buying us ice cream cones near one of Papi's
cafés. Mami wanted to see her brother, Café Aroma's main
shop manager in Bayamo, so we wandered over after ice
cream. He was out. Mami had our driver take us home.
Later in the day we ate dinner in silence. Mami's eyes were
red, and her hands were shaking as she held her fork. I
didn't really taste dinner.

The silence was getting to me. Tony wandered off –
probably to watch television. I finally spoke, "Mami it's
almost dark. I am getting worried."

"*Mi hija* I'm sure your father will be very careful.
He knows what he is doing," she said.

Just then Tony ran back into the dining room and
yelled, "I hear Papi's Oldsmobile" and kept running towards
the front door. Mami and I jumped up and ran to the door
to greet them.

Papi and J.J. looked very tired and pale when they walked in. Papi kissed us all and handed me a sprig of a coffee plant with the white flowers still on it. He gave Tony a small bag of coffee beans "For your experiments," said Papi with a wink. He looked at Mami and said, "Everything is fine. We will talk later. J.J. and I need to eat something."

Mami ordered the cook to bring in two plates, and we all sat at the dining table. Papi did all of the talking.

"The farm looks good. Your brother, Manolo, thinks we are going to have a great harvest this year. It hasn't rained too much, and the guerillas stay off our lands for the most part. I guess the protection money is paying off."

"We took some horses out and rode along the fences. Everything looks secure," said Papi.

"Papi I am tired. I think I'll head off to bed," said J.J. "I'm going to read for awhile. Goodnight everyone."

Tony and I rose to follow, but Mami asked us to sit still. "I know you guys are eager to quiz J.J., but he truly looks tired. Leave him be till the morning. Go off and watch some television. It's almost time for your favorite show, Gabi, Fofo y Miliki Comedy Hour," she said.

18 August 1958

J.J. was up early today. Tony and I found him in the backyard playing with our dog Paton (big foot). At first he kept throwing the ball to Paton, over and over. Then he looked over at us and motioned for us to follow him away from the house and down the street a bit. We sat under a mango tree at the corner and listened to his story.

"Papi was amazing yesterday. Some of Castro's men must have spotted the car. Maybe he has spies at the farm.

"It was shortly after lunch when some of his men arrived. They motioned for Papi to follow them into the woods. Papi held his ground and said they could state their business in front of us – Tio Manolo and me.

"Castro's men dress in olive drab uniforms and wear flattened hats. There were four of them. And, all of them carried guns at their hips in holsters.

"One of the men approached Papi and asked him where August's payment was. He had one day left to pay or his cattle ranch would be set on fire. They had already placed gasoline drums around the warehouse where Papi stores the bulk of the raw coffee beans from the mountain farm before they are processed.

"The men now wanted an additional $1,000 on top of the $10,000 Papi pays monthly.

"Papi was furious! He walked closer to their leader and informed him that he had already paid $10,000 to Boniato back on August 5th. He remembers the day clearly because his nephew was killed a few hours later in a car wreck."

Tony stopped J.J. during his story and asked, "Who is Boniato?"

"Boniato is a nickname given to one of Castro's assassins. He works out of Santiago. They say he is brutal. I don't know who gave him the nickname because he's definitely not a sweet yam. Papi says he is a sadistic killer and would never cross him.

"Anyway, Papi went on to tell this guy that he had one day to remove the gasoline drums from around his property. He also told him that if Tio Miguel and his family are harmed in any way, there will be hell to pay.

"I guess the guy believed Papi because he didn't press him for many details and left with his posse shortly after.

"Papi looked at me and said, 'it is just beginning. You wait and see. Just wait and see.' Then, he walked back to his offices and left Tio Manolo and me in the field."

That was the gist of J.J.'s story of their day at the farm. He is such a good storyteller that Tony and I did not have many questions. J.J. seems older today. Maybe it's just my imagination.

19 August 1958

I can tell J.J. is worried. He usually loves to spend his days reading. Today I catch him staring off into space. He walks aimlessly around the house. He won't sit in front of the television to watch any shows. Tony asked him to walk to the park and play some baseball, but J.J. said no. Later Tony dropped a garden snake in J.J.'s lap, and J.J. hit him. I can't remember the last time J.J. did something like that. He's almost 16 and very mature for his age – or so he says to us.

Fabuloso stopped by for a lesson, but my heart just wasn't into it. I kept messing the steps up. I lost my balance. I didn't hear what the teacher or Fabuloso said to me. Fabuloso asked me what was wrong, but I didn't want to talk about it. Papi is his father's business partner, and I don't think I should be discussing these things with him. I eventually said I had a headache and asked to be excused.

I've actually never had a headache in my life, but Mami gets migraines all of the time. Mami is short already, especially next to Papi. Papi is tall and normally towers over the other men in a room. Whenever Mami's head hurts she looks even shorter. Her shoulders hunch over and looks stooped like Mama Aurora, my 90 year old great grandmother. When Mami gets a headache she retreats to her bedroom with the curtains closed tight over the windows.

That is what I did today. I went to my bedroom and sat in the dark. I'm worried about Papi, the family and the farm. Papi left early this morning, and I think he's checking out all of his properties in Bayamo – the cattle ranch, Café Aroma, the headquarters next to the ranch that house all of the equipment to clean, shell and toast the coffee beans.

21 August 1958

Yesterday we rode together to the cattle ranch to visit Tio Miguel and the family. Everyone climbed into Papi's green Olds. Papi loves to drive. He loves to brag about how he made his first million before the age of 21 on horseback. He says that in America teenagers can drive. Here in Cuba we must wait until 21 to apply for our driver's license. Women rarely drive. Mami has a driver assigned to her because she never learned. Papi is nostalgic about picking up huge bags of coffee beans and tying them on a horse then traveling down the Sierra Maestra to deliver them to town. But, now he has a fleet of trucks with the company logo.

Tio Ricardo, Tia Dolores and the girls came too. Tio Ricardo is still very quiet. He sat with us most of the day. He is trying to resume some of the operations on his ranch. Papi and Tio talked business for awhile.

Tia is smoking now! I could tell Mami was scandalized. Tia Dolores said the doctor recommended it for calming her nerves down. She says it keeps her hands busy and takes the edge off. Mami and Papi don't smoke, and I know they think it's awful when a woman smokes. Mami caught me sneaking a cigarette with my cousin Margarita from Cienfuegos, and she made me smoke the entire thing as I coughed and sputtered. Margarita thinks I'm a goody two shoes and doesn't want to come back for a visit next summer. It's my turn anyway to visit, but I don't want to go now.

Papi and J.J. searched the entire property with Tio. If Papi came here yesterday he sure didn't act like it. I have a feeling he sent some men to check things out and verify that the drums were removed by dusk last night because he seemed very confident as they left the house for a walk. Mami told Dolores, the cousins and us a watered down version of J.J.'s story. I wonder if she knows the truth or if she's hiding things from all of us. I don't think Papi would have brought us here unless he was satisfied with our safety and the safety of all of his properties. I guess things are okay for now.

30 August 1958

There is less than a week before my big day! I had my final fitting today at Tienda Gloria. The dress reminds me of a meringue. It starts off skinny at the top and grows out from there. It's pure white with pearls and crystals sewn on the bodice. I'm wearing long white gloves since the dress only has small cap sleeves. Mami wants me to wear a tiara too. She says Papi would really like that since he calls me his princess. I feel silly.

I can't wait to see Fabuloso in his tuxedo. He's been great during all of our practices. I think he likes me. He calls me Bella (beautiful) instead of Daniela. Mami and Papi think he would be a good match for me in the future. My parents did not have an arranged marriage, but it's not unheard of still in this day and age.

Mami loves to tell us the story of how they met and courted. She was 21 and visiting a friend for the day on the outskirts of Bayamo. Her friend lived on a smaller farm with her parents. Papi had some business with the friend's father and drove up in his first Café Aroma truck and came upon Mami sitting on the porch. He later told Mami he saw only her huge eyes and beautiful smile and was immediately smitten.

Papi showed up a few days later at Mami's house and asked her father for permission to court her. They would go on long walks with a sister or cousin as chaperone. They would sit on the porch in the early evening for hours. Mami laughs every time she thinks about Papa Tato stacking pillows in between them as they sat on a bench on the front porch. Mami blushes when she says as soon as Papa Tato would go back inside the house Papi would lean over the pillows and give her a quick kiss.

Mami always says Papi is a good man. That one day I will understand. That he doesn't follow the customs of most Cuban men and keep someone on the side. I already understand. When I see my cousin Margarita every summer she tells me about her father's mistress. How it is driving her mother slowly crazy. Her mom smokes too, and her father finds it disgusting. I sometimes feel bad for Margarita. She doesn't have brothers or sisters, and her parents are always fighting.

Fabuloso graduated last year from the same boarding school J.J. attends. He's almost 18 and talks about medical school. His father wants him in the family business and is refusing to pay for more school until Fabuloso works in the business for one year. If at the end of one year he is miserable, then he will be sent to La Habana to attend medical school.

7 September 1958

My feet ache! Last night was wonderful and scary.

We arrived an hour early to make sure everything was set up. The Club Deportivo has a huge restaurant area. It is a grand salon overlooking the pool. The pool looked beautiful. There must have been ten flower arrangements floating – each with a candle lit in the center. The table arrangements have calla lilies (my favorite), hibiscus and roses. Papi paid the house band so we will have live music tonight instead of records. I like records myself, but Papi wants the best for his princess. When Mami was satisfied with everything she said it was time for us to go to another room and wait for Fabuloso and his family. Fabuloso and I have to make a big entrance tonight once everyone is seated for dinner.

Mami took us to a smaller room she had also reserved and checked my hair, dress, earrings and makeup again. This is the first time I've worn lipstick and blush – if you don't count all the times I sneaked into Mami's bathroom and bedroom to play dress up.

Papi handed me a small box with a gold ribbon. I opened it up and found a beautiful heart shaped ring in eighteen carat gold with a pearl in the center of the heart and a thick gold bracelet, also in eighteen carat gold, with a gold coin charm. I gave Mami and Papi a huge hug and kiss each. I will always treasure these special gifts.

Mami and Papi look great tonight. Papi is in a tuxedo. Even Tony and J.J. got tuxedos for the event. Mami is wearing a strapless, shiny gold dress. Her hair is pulled back, but she has left some curls around her face. Mami says I look great too. She's happy because I gave in to the tiara. My hair is pulled off my face but hanging long in back.

Mami was very upset when Señor Federico, Señora Georgina and Adan walked in. She was gracious to everyone then turned to me and asked if I still needed to go to the bathroom and gave me THE LOOK. Mami's look is famous. When she turns her eyes on us we melt inside. She was fuming when we got to the bathroom and practically yelled, "How dare she wear a white dress!"

"Mami it's cream colored not white," I responded.

"She should know better. The debutante always wears white on her special day. Did you see how much cleavage that woman is showing? She shouldn't have bothered wearing anything at all," she said.

"Fabuloso looks dashing. I've never seen him so dressed up," I said.

"Yes. Let's get back there. You need to pin on his white rose. And, I think he was carrying some flowers for you," she said. Mami seemed much calmer now.

When we got back to the room only Fabuloso and Papi were left. They were talking and laughing. Fabuloso said his parents had wandered off to the bar for a drink and asked if I cared for anything from the bar. He is such a gentleman!

The rest of the evening was a blur. I was announced and came in to the grand salon on Fabuloso's arm. We had our first dance to "El Reloj" (the clock), a romantically slow song, and sat for dinner amid clapping. Papi went all out with the menu, and we had escargot, steak, lobster. Again Fabuloso and I danced, but this time we were joined by others. Mami and Papi came out to the dance floor. They were beaming with pride as I spun around. My friends from school and cousins were all there. I danced my heart out all night long.

Only Tio Ricardo and Tia Dolores didn't come. Papi didn't expect them to come after the death of Nando a month ago. Still it would have been nice to see them. Nando's favorite song came on, a Beny Moré song about a falling cigar, and I decided to walk out to the pool for some air. I must have had tears in my eyes because Fabuloso followed me out and held me. Just held me. It was the first time I had been in a man's arms when not dancing, except for Papi, of course. It was nice.

"Bella, are you okay?" asked Fabuloso.

"Yes. It's just that this song makes me sad. Nando loved to dance this one," I replied.

He was quiet for a while. Then he said, "I will give you a new memory for this song."

I looked up at him, and Fabuloso kissed me on the lips. He pulled away from my face and looked at me. This time I wasn't as surprised when his lips met mine again. My cousin Margarita says her first kiss felt like being struck by lightning. I definitely heard some fireworks – like Tony was setting off bottle caps. This time Fabuloso pulled away from me roughly and yelled, "*Mierda* (shit). Let's get inside fast."

I was confused. Fabuloso was running for the salon and dragging me by the hand. Another couple that had been outside was running. I saw Tony and J.J. running from behind the pool house. Tony had a funny expression on his face and kept blowing kisses in my direction. They must have been spying on me! *Cabron*! Bastard!

Inside everyone was standing away from the windows and toward the back of the room where the band would normally play. They must have taken a break after Nando's song. Once Papi saw that we were all inside he walked up to the stage and picked up a microphone. "Thank you for coming. The night is not over. The band still has one more set to play, but I, Daniela and the family understand if you choose to leave. Please drive home carefully and don't venture out past the Bayamo city limits. The Guardia has become nervous and strict. They will shoot first and ask questions later if they suspect you of moving weapons to the Sierra Maestra.

"You took a big chance coming here tonight. Thank you again for joining us to celebrate Daniela's fifteenth birthday. I had hoped the biggest event of the evening would have been my beautiful daughter walking into the room. It looks like either Batista or Castro is upstaging my family. Please enjoy the rest of your evening." Papi looked tired as he handed the microphone to the singer. The band was returning to the stage and the shooting was over – for now.

"J.J. you haven't danced with your sister all night", said Papi. "Mami let's go out onto the dance floor. I'll be damned if this night is ruined," he said under his breath.

9 September 1958

Papi found out today that Juan and Silvia Castillo were shot on their front porch by Castro's men. According to local gossip, the Castillos had a son in the Maestra that had become a guerilla. Their only son, Carlos, was an outcast and weirdo. Carlos had never had friends as a young child, and the Castillos mainly kept to themselves. Their neighbors had begun to feel like the Castillos were spying on them and reporting back to Carlos.

Papi's contacts in the Guardia say that Carlos was moving weapons for Castro and using his parent's home as the dropping point. According to the *capitán*, the Guardia intercepted a big cache of guns outside of Bayamo. They think Carlos was blamed for the missing weapons. Instead of executing Carlos, Castro's men drove past the Castillos emptying out their weapons and killing the couple as they enjoyed the nice evening. Castro loved to teach lessons, and this must have been one of them. Carlos is only 19. He must be terrified.

12 September 1958

J.J. leaves for Camaguey tomorrow. School starts up for us all on the fifteenth. We normally all ride up together, spend the night in Camaguey, drop J.J. off at school and head home. I was wondering what would happen after Nando's death and the shots fired during my birthday party, but Papi beat me to my question by announcing that everyone should start packing.

That night after dinner J.J. asked Mami to play the piano. She is an incredible piano player. All of her sisters are too. They took mandatory lessons as children, but Mami really excelled. Her younger sister, Virginia, plays the guitar. She visits us all of the time because she was never able to have children and has "adopted" Tony, J.J. and me as her own. We haven't seen her much since Nando's death. I really miss the music in the house. I didn't realize that J.J. did too.

Mami thought for a moment then said, "It's been more than a month since Nando died. I don't think it would upset God if I played some music now." She must have played for forty five minutes. It was nice. I noticed that every house has a heart beat and ours must be the piano. Mami would not be Mami without her Wulitzer baby grand piano that Papi gave her when J.J. was born.

14 September 1958

We are back from Camaguey. It was an uneventful trip. We passed a few Guardia Civil patrols on the road. We saw a few structures that had burned to the ground – probably because of all the civil unrest. But, overall things seem relatively unchanged. J.J. seemed relieved as we left and waved goodbye. Mami was teary eyed as we drove past the school's gate.

Tony and I start school tomorrow. I guess it will be nice to see some of my friends, but I don't really like school. I'm not as studious as J.J. I'm not the practical joker Tony is – always getting in trouble for one thing or another – but having a great time of it. I'm just an average student who enjoys a joke now and then.

I haven't heard from Fabuloso since my party. I wonder how he is doing. He must be busy working for his dad.

20 September 1958

Tony and I are home for our afternoon nap before we return to school. The house is especially quiet today. Mami has a migraine, so the curtains are closed, there is no music playing.

School is fine. I enjoy my writing and reading studies more than arithmetic. Tony is a whiz at everything. He can fix things, and he loves animals too. He says he wants to be a veterinarian when he grows up. J.J. is destined for architecture. His drawings are so precise. He spends hours on sketches of buildings or machines. I have no idea what I will study. Mami has her degree in teaching, but I think she really wanted to be a concert pianist before she married. Papi is an entrepreneur. He is great with arithmetic and keeps his own books.

I don't know what I will do. Maybe I will follow in Mami's footsteps and get my teaching degree and hope that I marry young. Mami is certified to teach English. If Papi studied English in school, he doesn't remember any now. Luckily, the three of us have had some English classes.

I like riding horses and have one at the cattle ranch called Chocolate. He's a beautiful chestnut and stands sixteen hands high. I'm just okay at ballet and piano. Again, Mami wants me to study these things so that I am an "accomplished" girl, but I'm not really good at any of those things. I can barely sew embroidery work. Thank God Mami has a cook. That's one thing I don't have to learn.

I wonder if Papi sees Fabuloso at work sometimes. Papi is always off visiting one store or another, the farms and the facility where they prepare the coffee. Tonight I will

ask Papi to take me to the Aroma Warehouse Facility
tomorrow.

21 September 1958

We had a beautiful Sunday! After mass, Papi took us to the
main Aroma Warehouse located about thirty minutes
outside Bayamo proper. This is where Papi has a huge
coffee bean warehouse and where the beans are cleaned,
shelled and sorted before shipment to the toasting facilities,
tostaderos, throughout Cuba.

Papi loves to tell us about the preparation of the
coffee from raw beans to finished product for sale at the
market or in his cafés. The fresh picked beans come to him
red or light brownish in color. He grows the bulk of them
high in the Sierra Maestra on his *cafetal*, a 130 acre
plantation, and supplements his crops with some purchases
locally. Most of the beans that are grown on his *cafetal* are
brought down on mules. The warehouse where Papi stores
the huge burlap bags of raw beans is at least the size of five
churches placed side by side.

Papi first washes the beans in huge vats where the
water drains through different levels down to a funnel. The
washed beans are allowed to dry in the sun, spread out for
hours on huge conveyer belts that are wider than a train is
long. Even though he has machines that pick out inferior
beans, he also employs workers to walk among the conveyor
belts and pick out anything that looks defective.

Once the beans are dried they are brought back
inside the warehouse and sent down a huge chute. The
beans are machine shelled and sorted by size. The shelled
beans now appear to be darker brown than when they first
arrived. Smaller chutes direct the sorted beans into large
bags with the Aroma logo. The bags are sewn shut and
weighed before being loaded unto trucks.

The trucks transport all of the bags to the main Aroma *Tostadero* right outside of Bayamo's city limits. The *tostadero* is located right near the train yard. The bags of coffee are either loaded onto trains or other trucks bound for every major city and province in Cuba or the bags are brought inside for roasting.

The Aroma Warehouse is closed on Sundays, so we had the place virtually to ourselves. While Mami and Papi inspected the machines and offices, Tony and I made our way out back to where they discard the shells. When the machines are running, the shells drop out of a huge chute at the top of the warehouse and fall into the yard. The yard is an enormous area surrounded by an eight foot concrete wall. The noise is unbearable during the day. Today it was quiet. And, there were several large mounds of shells since the workers clean the yard out on Wednesdays.

We climbed the iron steps that were anchored to either side of the cement wall and looked out at the sea of shells before us. Tony and I looked at each other and dove right in. This was much better than swimming at the club or even the ocean. We had our own private pool of coffee shells. We dove over and over into the shells until we were exhausted.

Later on I begged Papi to take us to the *tostadero*, but Mami and Papi were ready to head home. Besides, they wanted to stop in on Tio Ricardo and Tia Dolores on the way home and see how they are getting along without Nando. Tia Dolores is now chain smoking. She has lost so much weight. Tio Ricardo is steadily improving. His work on the farm keeps him busy and his mind off Nando. He is still worried about Dolores. The oldest girl has taken over the management of the house and staff. He says that Tia will wander around all day. Sometimes he gets in from the stables and finds her in Nando's bedroom.

I am sad now. Goodnight diary. You help me sleep without nightmares. I wonder if Tio and Tia have bad dreams at night. I wonder if Mami and Papi think often of Nando. I was his closest cousin and he mine. We shared a passion for riding horses and dancing. I miss him.

4 October 1958

It took Papi over a week to take us to the *tostadero*. He's been very busy at work again. He doesn't talk like he used to about his business. I think he is worried. I overheard him tell Mami yesterday that Batista's men are asking for money again.

If it's not one side of the revolution it's the other asking for something. Papi wants to remain neutral throughout all of this, but I know he is happy under Batista. Papi understands dictators and how they work – essentially for bribe money. Castro is an unknown force, and he doesn't like unknowns. He wants to protect his family, livelihood and business above all things.

We left for the *tostadero* Saturday morning right after breakfast. Mami and Papi always have *café con leche* in the morning and prefer plain café after lunch and dinner. So, their plan is for us to spend the morning at the *tostadero*, eat our picnic lunch and finish the meal off with a hit of Papi's freshly roasted café. Mami makes the best café – with lots of sugar, but we don't tell him that. Papi makes it too strong. We drink his and then wait for the opportunity for Mami to make another pot. He would die if he knew this!

There is no better smell in the world than that of the *tostadero*! Papi has them all over Cuba, but the one in Bayamo is the biggest. The beans are placed in the largest cooking pan I've ever seen. It's probably bigger than our living room at home. The coffee beans are slow roasted, and the smell is indescribable. You can smell it from a couple of blocks away.   The roasted beans are then placed in cellophane bags and transported to the market and cafés for sale.

Tony and I wandered off on our own to explore. We eventually found a room where Café Aroma stored the float from this summer's parade. We had so much fun in July for the city wide festival. It seems like so long ago. Tony rode in the car that pulled the float while a bunch of my girl cousins, friends and I had dressed up and waved to the crowds from behind. The float played a recording of Papi's radio commercial song. Tony and I began to sing, "*Tomen señores Café Aroma y usted verá. Tomen señores Café Aroma y le gustará.*" (Drink Café Aroma and you will see. Drink Café Aroma and you will like it.) We kept goofing around and changed it to, "*Tomen señores Café Aroma de mi papá.*" The lyrics stuck in our heads.

We drove Mami and Papi crazy as we rode home singing, "*Tomen señores Café Aroma de mi papá.*" It eventually stuck in their minds too. It's become the new family motto.

11 October 1958

Today is J.J.'s 16th birthday. Papi has asked him not to come home because the fighting has intensified this month. He fears the roads are not safe for travel.

It has been three years since Castro made his way up the Sierra Maestra and ensconced himself for the long fight. In September of 1955, he left Mexico with some allies and buddies who had sworn him allegiance and arrived by boat near Manzanillo. Papi says that Castro grows more impatient by the day. His guerillas are gaining strength and attacking Batista's Guardia more consistently.

Mami had planned a small celebration for J.J. She has decided to still have the party and call him during the party to sing him *Feliz Cumpleaños*. Lots of cousins, aunts and uncles are coming over for lunch in our courtyard. She asked Papi to invite Fabuloso and family over too. I wonder if he will come. He hasn't made an effort to call or visit since my birthday party. I have butterflies in my stomach. I don't know if I'll be able to eat any of the food the cook has prepared – empanadas, ham croquettes, mini sandwiches with pimento or asparagus spread, roasted pork, congris (black beans and rice) and fried plantains.

I need to go get ready and help Mami with table settings, flowers and music.

(Later on)

He came! Fabuloso looked so handsome in his white *Guayabera* shirt. I think he's taller. He came alone. Mami winked at me and seated us together for lunch.

"How have you been Bella?" asked Fabuloso. "I've missed our dance practices," he continued.

I probably turned a brighter shade of red than a tomato and replied, "I've missed you too. I've been busy with school, the usual." Then I asked, "How is the job with your father?"

"It's not as bad as I imagined it to be. It's just that I'd rather be saving lives than determining inventory needs," he said.

Mami brought out J.J.'s birthday cake and placed a call to his school. He was waiting in the headmaster's office, so we all began to sing immediately.

I never did work up the nerve to ask Fabuloso why he hadn't called or visited since September. I hope I don't have to wait another month to see him again.

20 October 1958

Gunfire is becoming a nightly occurrence. It never really gets close to the house, but it's frightening just the same. I'm glad there is a curfew after dark. I don't want anyone else in my family getting hurt.

Tio Ricardo, Tia Dolores and my cousins came over for Sunday brunch yesterday after mass. Tia was absent at mass. Mami asked her if she was feeling well and Tia replied, "I don't believe in God anymore. What purpose do I have at mass? If there was a God, Nando would still be alive."

Mami was quiet for a moment then she said, "Dolores, I can't begin to understand what you must feel right now. The pain must be overwhelming. But, I believe God has His reasons for everything He does."

"And, what would that reason be? Tell me why your God would take my Nando away from me at 22 years of age? Tell me," said Dolores.

"I don't know," said Mami. Her words were barely above a whisper.

14 November 1958

We are going away for the weekend! Papi is taking all of us to Santiago. Even J.J. is invited to join us. Papi says the train from Camaguey to Santiago should only take three hours or so. J.J. is undecided because exams are coming up soon, and he has a lot of studying. Normally Papi would drive us, but he wants to take our driver Yayo tomorrow.

Papi has ordered the latest Ford truck for his fleet of delivery vehicles. If one is ready, he wants to drive it back to Bayamo and surprise Tio Miguel. Tio Miguel's knee is on the mend. He's using a cane to walk and has a slight limp. Overall the knee healed well after the surgery. Tio has taken over his duties at Papi's cattle ranch again, and Papi wants to show him the latest and greatest truck. Papi says Miguel hasn't driven since Nando died, and it's time to get him back in the saddle.

Mami and I plan to get some shopping in too while we are there. Santiago is the second largest city in Cuba, so we always find great things in the stores. We'll probably stay with one of Mami's sisters in Vista Alegre. They both live in a beautiful part of Santiago. I'm sure that both Tia Carolina and Tia Eva will join us for some shopping.

16 November 1958

The weekend didn't turn out as expected. J.J. stayed at boarding school to study. Mami got a migraine when we arrived and had to cancel the shopping portion of our trip. And, the truck Papi ordered wasn't quite ready.

Since Mami was under the weather and I was bored, Papi offered to take me to the Ford dealership. Papi's driver, Yayo, dropped us all (Papi, Tony and me) off at Carretera Central in front of the Agencia Principal de Autos y Camiones (Ford dealership). Papi knows the manager, Señor Angel de Leon, very well because they have done business for years. Señor de Leon is very nice and excited to show us an example of the C-900 that Papi has ordered. Unfortunately, not one of the trucks is ready for Papi because he has a special paint job done at the factory. His personal cars are almost always Oldsmobiles and always painted a medium green, like the color of the sea. But, his coffee business is strictly red. Not a bright red – more of a burgundy color. He has his own paint color that no one else can use specially mixed for his fleet. Señor de Leon says that they are waiting for more paint to complete the job at the factory. But, he welcomes Papi to look at a black truck he has in stock.

I'll have to ask Papi why he chose red for his businesses. I know how much he loves the sea and the color green. When we go to the beach at Guardalavaca and stay at the Hotel Lala, Papi spends all of his time in the water. He taught us all to swim since he is a very strong swimmer in the ocean. He'll go out so far he looks like a speck on the horizon. I rarely see him swim at the Club. He says he's strictly an ocean man and doesn't particularly like pools. Papi has purchased an empty lot on our favorite beach. He plans to begin construction of a beach house next summer once things settle down.

Señor de Leon motions us to follow him to the showroom floor. On the way he introduces us to his son, Julian, who helps out on the weekends in the dealership. Julian is very good-looking. I think he's J.J.'s age with dark hair and eyes and a great tan. Julian offers to get us some sodas. Tony and I say yes and follow the men. Señor de Leon opens the door of the black C-900 and asks us to get in. He says these are heavy duty trucks and sold on an order basis only. They don't keep extra stock.

Julian comes back with our sodas as his father is explaining some of the features to us. Señor de Leon can tell that I'm bored and offers to have Julian show me around. I wait for Papi's permission and follow Julian around the showroom. He takes me back towards the offices and eventually to the area where they service and clean cars.

"I just love cars. I come here every weekend and wash cars or help the mechanics out," says Julian. "Do you like cars," he asks me.

"I guess I never really thought about it. Our driver takes us to school and back twice a day. Papi drives us to mass on Sundays. Other than that, I'm not usually in a car. I wish I could just ride my horse, Chocolate, around town," I reply. I ask him, "Do you have a horse?"

Julian replied, "No. Are you a millionaire or something?" Then he nicknames me Reina (queen) and starts to slowly walk me back towards the showroom where Papi and Señor de Leon are still talking.

"So, Reina, do you live in Santiago?" he asks.

"No. I'm from Bayamo," I reply.

"Jeez. I've heard the fighting is pretty bad there. Why doesn't your rich daddy move you someplace safer, Reina?" He continues, "I'm sure you've got plenty of money to live anywhere in Cuba."

"First of all, my name is Daniela, not Reina! And, secondly, it's none of your business how wealthy my dad is," I yell.

I've never been so rude in my life, and I gasp. I can tell my face is bright red. I start to walk away from Julian, and he grabs my hand and pulls me back towards him.

"Listen. I was out of line. I'm sorry. Will you let me brew you some café? We carry only the best, Café Aroma," he says.

I start to laugh and reply, "Sure."

I never did tell Julian who we are. I'm sure he'll be surprised when his father tells him our last name. I guess I had the last laugh. He was pretty cute.

I asked Papi about the red cars and trucks for his business, and he said he likes the color red and if he really had to think about it, coffee is in his blood – hence the red paint job.

29 November 1958

Another month has passed and still no call or visit from Fabuloso. There are no interesting boys at school. I find myself thinking a lot about Julian and Fabuloso both. I wish I had a sister to talk to.

Tony is a great kid, but he drives me crazy. Yesterday, he took his goat, Terri, for a walk and let it off the leash. We heard some frantic knocking in the evening and Papi answered the door. The fire department was at our door, and before they could even speak Papi turned to us and yelled, "Tony!"

Sure enough Terri had gotten on the roof of our neighbor's house across the street. This is the third time Tony has let this happen. Our neighbors are older, probably in their seventies, and every time Terri gets on the roof they think someone is walking around and get terrified. I don't know if Tony is careless or just wants attention.

Papi is fed up, and sends Tony off to his room for bed early, but, not before informing us that tomorrow we are going to Jiguaní. Papi has had enough of Terri and is shipping him off to his brother's farm about forty minutes from Bayamo in Jiguaní. His brother, Jorge, raises chickens, goats, sheep, pigs and a few cows. It's a small farm, probably only forty acres, but we have a family reunion there every year because it's about halfway between Bayamo and Santiago. Tony looks stricken. Frankly, I think it serves him right for being so irresponsible.

7 December 1958

This is worse than Nando's death! Papi was picked up yesterday morning by the Guardia Civil!

We had just finished breakfast at around eight o'clock when there was a knock at the door. One of the maids must have answered because within seconds two of Batista's men were in the dining room. They asked Papi to come with them.

Mami asked, "Where are you taking my husband?"

"We have orders to pick him up and deliver him at the central station in Holguín, señora," replied one of the men.

"Holguín! Why take him almost two hours away from here," she demanded.

"Look señora, we do not know any more. You can call Holguín yourself and ask for *Comandante* Guerro. He should know what is going on," he said.

Mami turned to Papi and said, "Don't worry. I'm going to call your lawyer right away."

Papi looked at us all and said, "Don't be frightened. I'm sure there is some misunderstanding. I'll be back right away."

It was a Friday and we had school, but Mami thankfully kept us home. Now, it has been a day and a half and we haven't heard anything about Papi. Mami immediately called Holguín, but wasn't told any more than we already knew. Papi's lawyer is in La Habana right now. I'm not sure he could help anyway. His business is contracts, real estate and civil law.

Mami puts up a brave front, but we know she's very upset. She keeps going to the front window every few minutes. She hasn't played the piano since Papi left. And, she can't sit still. This waiting game is driving us crazy! At least with Nando, we had news right away. This unknown, this waiting can kill a person.

8 December 1958

Papi is home now. He's not saying much about what happened in Holguín. Only that there was a mix up with some payments he gave to Batista's men. He doesn't want to talk about it.

13 December 1958

J.J. got home yesterday afternoon! His final exams are over for the semester, and he has the rest of the year off. Tony and I finished school today too. We don't go back until January 12th. It's so nice to have a whole month off from studies.

Shortly after J.J. arrived, Mami and Papi sat us down in the living room. They wanted to tell us about what happened in Holguín as a family. Papi asked us to listen without questioning him. This was Papi's story.

"Your mother doesn't want me to tell you what happened in Holguín, but I think you all need and deserve to know.

"Every month I pay Batista $10,000. This is my price for protection. It allows me to keep my businesses running smoothly. I have been paying him off for years, but since Castro started to cause problems my protection price has escalated. The first week of the month one of his men stops by my offices at the *tostadero*.

"This month the local *capitan* stopped by on the 5th, a little later than usual but not alarming. I gave him the cash and forgot about it. It's unpleasant but something I must do.

"The central office in Holguín had not received my payment by the morning of the 6th and sent the two local men you saw over right away to bring me in. They were very courteous and never mistreated me. They took me straight to the *comandante* in Holguín. Unfortunately, I cannot say that the *comandante* treated me with the same respect. He had me put in an interrogation room where I sat for what seemed like hours without food or water.

"Eventually he came in and said he had been busy preparing my noose. They were about to hang me for failing to make December's payment.

"I explained that I had indeed paid the *capitán* in Bayamo and that he should check with him immediately. At first he seemed not to believe me, but then he decided to go check on my story.

"Several more hours went by. I think I even slept some in my chair with my head on the table. The *comandate* returned at some point and said I was cleared to go.

Apparently, the local *capitán* called in sick on Friday and never sent a telegram to Holguín that the money had been collected. The *comandante* never did apologize for his error. And, he didn't have the decency to bring me back to Bayamo. Instead, he had a man drop me off at the train station. He practically threw me out of his office as he said, 'Hurry. You don't want to miss the last train.'

"I'm telling you this story because you need to know what is going on in Cuba. I don't know what will happen in the next few months. Things are bad – fighting, corruption, death. I wish I could spare you children from knowing these things, but you need to realize that we are in the middle of a revolution.

"We will continue to live our lives as we always have – minding our own business, taking care of our family, attending school and running Café Aroma – for as long as we can."

Papi is so brave! He refuses to let anything get him down. And, he wants us to be brave too.

We are leaving early tomorrow for Jiguaní. About eighty cousins, aunts, uncles, etc. are expected at Tio Jorge's farm for an early Christmas celebration. Family is coming from Santiago and Bayamo. It should be a great time.

15 December 1958

Well, yesterday started off amazingly well. We got to Tio Jorge's farm a little after ten o'clock in the morning. There were already several cars. Almost immediately Tia Celeste gave each of us jobs to do. J.J. was put in charge of directing traffic and getting cars parked. I got sent to the kitchen to help out. And, Tony was put in charge of guarding the growing tower of presents under the huge oak tree near the house. I got the crappiest job of all, but it was still fun to visit with my aunts and girl cousins in the kitchen. The smells of *congris* (black beans and rice), *yuca* and *boniato* (sweet yams) were delicious.

The men were outside roasting the pigs and goats that had been marinated in *mojo* (lemon juice and garlic). They were sitting in the shade on foldout chairs drinking Hatuey beer. I saw Papi sitting near Tio Jorge. Most of the men had on white or pastel *Guayaberas* and looked very handsome.

Tia Celeste had already set the tables outside. Every year she has Tio Jorge construct four long tables by placing barn wood on top of sawhorses. Then, they place bales of hay all around the tables. Each table easily seats twenty people. Tia Celeste makes everything look beautiful by using colorful fabrics and flowers. She is amazing.

Close to noon everyone had arrived and Tio Jorge said the blessing and welcomed everyone to start eating. Most of the "kids" sat together. I'm still not old enough to sit at the adult table, so I sat near some cousins. Margarita was there. Every time I took a bite of roasted goat she would say "baa-baa." At first it was funny, but then she started doing it when Tony took a bite of goat too.

I was getting upset and ran over to Tio Jorge to ask him if we were eating Terri today. One look said it all! Tony must have followed me over because I heard him sobbing behind me. What a *puta* (bitch). I wouldn't give Margarita the satisfaction of seeing me cry. Tony and I sat down. Neither of us ate much more that day. I noticed that Papi steered clear of the goat on his plate and only ate pork.

After lunch we had a huge gift exchange. Every Christmas we draw names for the following year. My Tia Dolores gave me a shawl that she had hand embroidered. It's beautiful. I was especially touched because she's been such a wreck since Nando's death. She told me that as much as she hates smoking, the tobacco has helped calm her nerves. Speaking of Nando, he must have chosen Margarita last year because I noticed she was the only one left without a gift. Tia Celeste noticed too and gave her one of the tablecloths from a picnic table. Ha!

Overall, it was a fun day – even if I did eat a piece of Terri. I think Tony has learned a temporary lesson. I'm sure he'll be up to his old tricks soon.

24 December 1958

Noche Buena! Christmas Eve! The best night of the year… at least I hope it will be this year.

There is still fighting in the streets, even though it's the holidays. Because of all the fighting, people are wary of traveling right now. Papi decided last week to invite any family and friends over tonight that want to come. Papi says Fabuloso and family will attend. I talked Mami into letting me wear a black velvet dress with a pearl necklace. She thinks I'm too young to wear black, but I think it looks great with my pale skin, dark eyes and black hair. We are expecting about thirty people tonight for dinner. Normally we go to midnight mass, but I wonder how the fighting will be tonight. If we hear lots of shooting, most likely we will stay at home.

25 December 1958

There was a lull in the fighting last night, so we all headed to mass at San Salvador after a wonderful evening. The food was delicious. Mami played the piano for everyone. And, we exchanged gifts. Mami and Papi had bought something for everyone.

On *Noche Buena* we traditionally receive one gift from Mami and Papi. Most of the gifts arrive from *Los Reyes Magos* (the Three Wise Men) on the day of the epiphany, January 6th. This year I got a new saddle for Chocolate. J.J.

got a drafting table for his room. And, Tony got a new goat! We were all laughing so hard. Tony calls her Terri Tambien (Also Terri). Papi told Tony he better keep Terri Tambien in our yard, or we would be feasting on goat soon. I think he feels pretty bad about Terri. I don't think Papi expected Tia Celeste to serve her up at the family reunion.

Fabuloso stayed by my side most of the evening. He said I lived up to his nickname for me, Bella, and said I was the prettiest girl at the party. Actually, I was the only girl at the party under 20, but I felt special anyway. I also finally worked up the courage to ask him about his unusual first name. I've never heard of anyone in Cuba named Adan before and only recognize the name from the bible – Adan y Eva. Fabuloso says his father wanted to go into the seminary as a teenager to study for the priesthood. He was the eldest of two boys, and his father decided he should instead go into the family business and that the younger brother would become the priest in the family. Now as the eldest, Fabuloso is being pushed into the family business too. He claims he's really trying to fulfill his father's wishes but he wants nothing more than to go to medical school in La Habana. He has already been accepted. Fabuloso says that by next fall he will make his final decision.

I was really surprised when Fabuloso pulled a small box out of his suit pocket for me. "Here you go Bella. Something beautiful for someone so beautiful," he said.

I was afraid to open the box. I didn't really know what to expect. Inside the box was an oval shaped, silver locket with filigree scroll work attached to a stick pin. "Thank you. I don't know if I should accept this. It's lovely," I said.

"Please accept it. I want you to wear it often and think of me," he said.

"What pictures should I put inside?" I asked.

"For now put your Mami and Papi. Maybe one day you can replace the pictures of your parents with pictures of us. Okay?" he asked.

"That sounds great. Thank you again," I replied.

I am so happy. I can almost forget the fighting on the streets at night during the last months – the gunshots, the curfews. I can't forget how Papi was kept prisoner for two days. Not knowing where he was made me more terrified than I've ever been in my life. And, there is still so much sadness and grief in my heart when I think about Nando's senseless death.

As we sat at mass tonight I tried to pray for Nando, for our family and for Cuba. Tia Dolores may be right; how could God allow these things to happen? I still recall how much I wanted to be a nun when I was in elementary school – how I was enthralled by statues of the Virgin Mary and Jesus. Now my heart feels heavy. Mami says the teenage years are the hardest years and that it will get better. But, I don't think Mami had to deal with the violence I've seen this past year. Sometimes I get really tired. It's hard to get up in the morning. Mami usually yanks me by the ear or pinches me and gets me moving again.

I'm going to sleep with my locket pinned to my pajamas tonight. Thank you Fabuloso!

Mami raised her eyebrows when she came in to kiss me goodnight. If Papi saw the locket, he didn't say anything. He has been so distracted lately. He tries so hard to keep up a heroic front for the rest of us, but I think he's scared too.

26 December 1958

Tia Virginia and Tio Enrique are staying with us right now. They came over for *Noche Buena* and haven't left. Apparently, Tio was at work in Papi's *tostadero* when some

men from the local police arrived at their house last week
and searched it from top to bottom. They wouldn't say what
they were looking for, but Tia did learn that one of the
guerrillas captured last week was named Pichardo. It's not a
very common name, so they have been searching the homes
of the two or three people in Bayamo with that last name.
What terrible luck for Tio and Tia to be named Pichardo.

Tia is terrified. She said that during their search
they dumped out drawers, yanked back curtains so hard
that the rods fell out of the walls and ripped open a sofa
with their knives.

Mami says Tia has become paranoid. She's afraid to
leave our house. She jumps at the slightest noise. And, Tia
won't play the guitar or sit with Mami at the piano. Mami
thinks it's only a matter of days before they leave the
country. Tia Virginia has been begging Tio to go to Miami.
She can't take the fighting anymore. Mami is really worried
about her. I'm worried too. My second mother seems so
depressed, and I don't know what to do to cheer her up.

27 December 1958

Today several aunts and uncles came over for lunch. Mama
Aurora and Papa Tato came too. Even Tia Caridad and Tio
Pedro are here – they moved to Miami last year because of
Tio's survey business. He got a big contract in the United
States. They've been visiting for a week now. They love it in
Miami and have convinced Tio Enrique that Tia Virginia
would be much happier there. It's become clear to everyone
that Tia Virginia is on the verge of collapse. I guess the
search of her house unhinged her. So, tonight they are
taking the train to La Habana and have booked a flight out
of Cuba on the 29th.

I am sad to see them go. Tia Virginia has been a
constant friend in my life. She acts more like a sister than an

aunt. Maybe next year they will come back for a visit.
Everything is changing so fast! I can't write fast enough to
keep up with the deaths, departures, fights…

30 December 1958

We got a call that Tio and Tia got on the plane safely. There
is still fighting at night. Every night the Guardia posts men
at the top of the bell tower of the church, San Salvador.
From there Papi says they can see the whole city and shoot
at anyone that looks suspicious. Sometimes soldiers climb
on rooftops. It's hard to tell if they are Guardia or guerrillas.
It's not safe to open your door after dark.

     J.J. doesn't sleep anymore. He has become so
worried about the fighting. There are guerrillas out there his
age who are fighting. He walks the house at night. I think
he fancies himself on security patrol. This insomnia is
getting to him though. He has become almost morose. He
was always quiet anyway. But, now all he talks about are
our family members on the ranches. He wonders if
everyone is doing okay. He wonders out loud if they've
been shot like Nando. Mami and Papi are really worried.
Tony and I are worried too. We've tried telling him jokes,
just talking to him, trying to get him outside during the day.
I don't think we're really helping.

31 December 1958

We are going to stay home tonight. For as long as I can
remember we've always gone to the club for New Year's
Eve. But, Mami and Papi fear it's just not safe this year. It's
been so crazy these last few months, especially these last few
weeks. We hear about men "disappearing." Hardly a night
passes that we don't hear shots fired.

     Earlier today one of Mami's nieces, Magdalena,
stopped by. She confessed to Mami that she has fallen in

love with one of Castro's men. A couple of months ago she was staying with Tio Manolo in the Sierra Maestra at Papi's *cafetal*. Tio told her a story about a "boy" who was staying on the neighboring farm. One of Castro's men had shot him for taking a can of condensed milk without permission. The guerrilla was nursing his wounds. The woman on the neighboring farm was *simpatico* (sympathetic) to Castro's cause and was helping him get better.

Magdalena asked Tio Manolo if she could visit the boy and bring him one of her comic books. She often reads her brother's leftovers. They became fast friends, and she would visit him often. His name is Rafael. This is the story Rafael told her.

"You have no idea how hungry we get sometimes. There are soldiers assigned to getting food for the rest of us. They go into town and buy what they can and steal the rest.

I came up to the mountains earlier last summer to join Castro because I was sick of the corruption in Cuba. Batista runs the country like a mobster not like a president.

I had no idea how violent Castro and his men could be. And, I hadn't considered things like food, water, clothes. I was stupid and young, only 17. My parents were devastated the day I left home, but I did what I thought was right in my heart.

A couple of months ago I was particularly hungry. We hadn't been given our daily rations. I saw a can of condensed milk sitting on a bench, and I just couldn't resist taking it. I opened it with my pocket knife and started drinking the milk. One of the *jefes* (bosses) came by and saw me, looked me directly in the eyes and walked past me. Castro must have been behind me, but I never saw him.

The *jefe* asked Castro in a loud voice, "What should I do with Rafael? I haven't given anyone permission to eat yet today."

Then Castro said, "Why don't you shoot him?"

Those were the last words I heard before a loud bang registered, and I felt a searing pain in my back. I think I passed out because everything is hazy after that.

I was lucky though. The bullet passed through my upper right back and out my chest. I've been here ever since. I'm almost completely healed now. I plan to walk home in a few days. I didn't want my mom and dad to see me until I was better."

Magdalena has been visiting him ever since. She says Rafael has turned his back on Castro and his men. He now realizes they are just as bad, if not worse, than Batista. His parents are relieved to have him home and have treated Magdalena like a family member. Rafael turned 18 in the mountains and wants a life with Magdalena.

Mami told me she thinks Magdalena is too young – also 18. But, she didn't try to discourage her from her love. Mami says that danger can bring people closer together. I definitely see that with our family. Tony and I fight less these days. The both of us are working together to get J.J. out of his funk. I think the three of us have been on our best behavior around Mami and Papi. We can sense how tense they are during these holidays.

1 January 1959

Happy New Year? The news is EVERYWHERE! Batista left the country last night at half past eleven on a plane bound for the United States. You can't turn on a radio or television without hearing or seeing the news. He flew out of La Habana and went to Daytona, Florida.

We are all in shock. It was so unexpected. Papi never thought he would walk away – just like that. Papi says that Batista has left in style and very wealthy. Papi is worried about the future now. Batista, for all of his problems, was a known quantity – somebody he could throw money at and make go away. He doesn't think Castro will be so easy to deal with.

4 January 1959

It has been impossible to write these last few days. All hell broke loose after the news of Batista's departure flooded the airwaves. Castro and his men have come down from the mountains, and it's pandemonium on the streets. The Guardia is not giving up without a fight. And, Castro is waging war around Cuba.

We were caught unprepared Friday the 2nd. Late in the afternoon Mami went down the street to run a few errands. She was near the church when the shooting started. A man she knew from the post office kept begging her to run. He tried to pull her towards the park and beckoned her to hide under a bench. Mami was too terrified to hide. Instead she started running. She says she jumped over some bushes and stayed as close as she could to the buildings. We heard shooting and were very anxious. Papi had left earlier that day to work at the *tostadero*. Now that Tio Enrique left for Miami, Papi needs to make sure he finds someone to handle his books at the office. So, we were home alone when the shooting started. J.J. made us go into the back bedroom. Thankfully, we didn't have to wait long for Mami to arrive. She was panting when she found us in the bedroom.

"Thank God you're alright," she yelled. "There is so much shooting out there," she continued.

"I think we should call Papi right away," said J.J.

"You're probably right J.J., but there are too many windows in between here and the phone. I think we need to stay put," said Mami. "We're safe and together," she continued.

We must have sat in the back bedroom for five hours. Tony hid in the armoire part of the time. When the fighting would get really intense we would flatten ourselves under the bed. It was well past dark and Papi was still not home. Mami was becoming frantic. She was desperate to call Papi at the *tostadero*, but she dared not leave us alone in the bedroom.

Papi got home around nine o'clock. He found us hiding in the bedroom and gave each of us a huge hug and a kiss.

"You have no idea what's going on out there," Papi said. "I think my car was hit by a stray bullet."

"I was near the bank when the fighting started," said Mami. "It was frightening."

"What! Are you okay," asked Papi.

"Other than a couple of grass stains on my dress, yes, I'm fine. At least physically. Now that you're here I need to sleep. I have the most awful migraine," said Mami. "What happened out there?" she asked.

"I was at the *tostadero* when I heard shots outside. I looked out of one of the office windows and saw four Guardia in a jeep chasing some men. I rounded up everyone in the offices, and we made our way back into the warehouse area. We stayed there most of the afternoon and evening," said Papi.

Mami asked, "Was Miguel there?"

"No. He didn't come in to work today. I gave almost everyone the day off. There were less than ten people at the *tostadero* today, thankfully," he said.

"How did you get home?" Mami asked.

"It was eight o'clock and the fighting had tapered off a bit. Everyone was getting restless, and we could hear the phones ringing in the front office. We all decided to go home. I dropped a couple of people off on the way home. Now, here I am," said Papi.

"What about the bullet hole?" Mami asked.

"At the corner of Jamaica and Marcano there was some shooting. I thought the car might have been hit. I'm not sure. It's dark," said Papi.

"This is crazy," said Mami.

Papi said he was starving and decided to go to the kitchen. Mami begged him not to go. There was still sporadic gun fire. Papi said he would be careful. We watched him crawl like an army soldier in a John Wayne movie down the hall. It was actually pretty funny, and we were all giggling. A few minutes later he returned, still on his stomach, pushing a plate of food. I've read that extreme stress can bring on all kinds of strange reactions – like laughing at a funeral. I'm not sure if we were all at the point of a breakdown, or if it was really funny. But, the laughing helped.

That night we all slept, or more like camped out, in the back bedroom.

The fighting was still bad the next day and even Sunday. We brought a radio and the television into the back bedroom, as well as, a couple of mattresses and some food. Mami and Papi also made lots of calls to check on family members. Everyone seemed to be holding up okay. They were scared but alive. What a crazy weekend!

5 January 1959

The fighting subsided a little today. There are still small pockets of resistance according to the news on the radio. Tio Ricardo and Tia Dolores brought Tio Pedro and Tia Caridad over to say goodbye. They heard on the radio that all American citizens should make their way to Guantanamo Naval Base. From there they will be sent home. Last year

they both became American citizens because they fell in love
with Miami and the United States. Now they are anxious to
leave Cuba and get back to their new home. Who can blame
them? I wonder if we will ever see them again.

6 January 1959

Dia de los Reyes Magos. The epiphany feast is usually a day
filled with presents, great food and family. Today we are
hiding in the shadows of our own home. There is still some
fighting, but each day that passes it gets quieter and quieter
on the streets. The radio says that the Guardia is falling
apart and resisting less and less. People have spotted Castro
in Bayamo out walking the streets.

Mami and Papi decided to stay home and didn't
invite anyone over because of all of the unrest. We had a
small dinner by ourselves and exchanged a few presents. It
was a somber day. Usually it's such a festive day. At least
we move around freely again within our home. We stay
away from the windows as much as possible. There hasn't
been any damage to windows or doors, but Papi says the
trim pieces and cornices around our roofline have bullet
holes and splintered pieces. It's a strange, strange world.

7 January 1959

Early this morning we heard bullhorns announcing that
Castro would be speaking at the town square at noon. A
little later a small group of people came by making music
with pots and pans and chanting, "*Uno, dos, tres y cuatro.
Fidel Castro para rato.*" (One, two, three and four. Fidel
Castro for awhile.)

We did not go listen to Castro today. We figured the
radio or news would cover his speech anyway. Instead,
Papi drove us to visit Tio Ricardo and Tia Dolores on their
farm. It was great to leave the house after our weeklong

"captivity." Surprisingly, the city isn't the worse for wear –
at least the part we drove through. Tio and Tia have been
fine on the farm. It looks like the city had it much worse.

We found out that when they delivered Tio Enrique
and Tia Virginia to Guantanamo day before last, the U.S.
Navy offered to fly them to Miami too, even though they are
not American citizens. Of course, they said no because they
have four girls still living at home. If only they had brought
them along. I hope they don't come to regret staying
behind.

When we got home Mami got a call from a man
under Castro's command. He told her to be ready, that
tomorrow a group of men were coming for lunch.
Unfortunately, Papi has work tomorrow at the *tostadero*, so
we will be home alone with Mami and the servants.

8 January 1959

The men arrived right before noon. There must have been
eleven or twelve of them. Mami immediately sent us into
the back bedroom but not before we could sneak a peek at
them.

We couldn't hear a word of what was said. But, we
didn't have to wait long to hear what had happened from
Mami. They ate and left within an hour.

Mami said they were dirty and smelly – dressed in
olive tones and drab uniforms. Most of the men had grown
beards similar to Castro and their hair desperately needed
trimming. They walked straight into the dining room and
leaned their rifles and machine guns along the walls behind
their chairs. Mami was terrified.

She said, "I have children in the house. Please place
your weapons on the floor pointing towards the back
window. My children are down that hallway over there,

and I don't want a gun inadvertently slipping down the wall and firing."

The men grumbled a bit about Mami's request. One of the men said, "I assure you that nothing like that will happen. We are just here at one of Fidel's houses to eat."

Mami replied, "You may call this Fidel's house, but those are my children. I don't want a gun to fire. Please."

One of the men stood up and did what Mami asked. Soon all of the men followed his example. And, Mami asked the cook to start bringing out all of the food. Mami had ordered the cook to prepare several legs of pork, *congris, yuca*, plantains and even a rice pudding for dessert. The men ate quickly and left. But, before they left they said, "There are lots of leftovers. We will be back."

While Mami was telling us the story someone knocked on our door. It was our next door neighbor and one of Mami's good friends, Mercedes. Mercedes said, "I see you had some company today. Are you all okay?"

Mami said, "Yes. We are fine. They called last night and said we needed to be ready to feed about a dozen men today."

"Did they behave decently?" asked Mercedes.

"We had some tense words about their weapons, but once they laid them on the floor I served the food, and there wasn't much conversation. I guess I prepared too much food though because they said they would be back tomorrow," said Mami.

"Listen. I don't have children and my husband is almost always home at lunchtime. Let's pack up all of the food. I'll take it with me. When I see the men approaching your house tomorrow I will intercept them and feed them myself," said Mercedes.

"No. I don't want to drag you into all of this. My husband is well known, and that is why they are doing this to us," said Mami.

Mercedes replied, "I insist. I can tell you are terrified. It's been thirty minutes since those pigs left, and you're still shaking all over."

Mami said, "You really don't mind?"

So, we all helped carry the food over to Mercedes' house. Poor Mami is a wreck. I can see she has a migraine, but she's not saying anything. I think she's so relieved that she doesn't have to feed Castro's men again.

9 January 1959

If Castro's men came back yesterday to eat we never saw them. Tony and I kept peeking out of the big front window when Mami wasn't looking, but we either missed them or they didn't come.

Castro has left Bayamo. He spoke in Santiago yesterday. And, there are news reports that he will be in Holguín tomorrow. It sounds like he's slowly making his way toward La Habana. At each major city, he's speaking and gaining popular support. Posters have started to appear too. The posters have slogans with Castro's name or even his picture.

There is almost no fighting today. Papi took J.J. to the *tostadero* this morning. Mami, Tony and I took a walk down our street and surveyed the damage. We even made our way toward the bank, post office, etc. As we see neighbors, friends and acquaintances, there are whispers of people who have disappeared. It is common knowledge that the police chief and Guardia chief here in Bayamo were assassinated. Most of Batista's men have surrendered, and the city is slowly returning to normalcy.

10 January 1959

Papi came home from the *tostadero* visibly upset. And, J.J. isn't talking at all. He was white as a sheet when he walked in. No one was talking. In fact, Papi sent us to bed early. I was bound and determined to find out what happened earlier in the day, so I stayed up after Mami and Papi kissed me goodnight.

As soon as I heard them go towards their bedroom I snuck out of my room with no shoes on and stood outside their door. I overheard Papi tell Mami that they witnessed a policeman get shot in cold blood by the railroad tracks near the *tostadero*.

Papi said, "It was a little after lunch and I took J.J. outside to inspect the buildings and parking lot. We happened to be near the railroad tracks when a jeep with three men pulled up to the other side of the track. They didn't even try to hide after they spotted us. The two men in front dragged their prisoner, a policeman, out of the jeep and made him kneel on the ground with his hands tied behind his back. Before I could react and at least turn J.J. around, they had shot the policeman at point blank range with a revolver."

I could hear Mami gasp.

Papi continued, "You should have seen J.J.'s face. He was so pale I thought he might pass out right there. I dragged him inside. As I was pulling him towards the *tostadero* one of Castro's men looked at me and smiled as if he had just kissed a baby instead of killed a man in cold blood."

Mami said, "There was nothing you could have done."

Papi replied, "It all happened so fast. I just hope J.J. isn't permanently damaged by what he saw. He becomes more nervous each day. It really worries me."

I went back to my room with tears streaming down my face. Since Nando's death, I really hadn't cried – not when Papi was imprisoned for a few days, not when we ate Terri, not when Tio and Tia left for America and not during all of the fighting of the past few weeks. Now I can't stop crying for my brother. I think I would have been shattered if I had seen an assassination. Poor J.J.!

13 January 1959

Castro is in La Habana. We are all sitting around the living room waiting for his victory parade to begin. There are plans to televise it live. We were supposed to start back to school yesterday, but things have literally been crazy. Papi thinks that by this weekend everything will be back to "normal."

What is normal after the last six months we have endured? And, I'm certain that Mami and Papi don't tell us the half of what is happening in Cuba. They want to shield us from the truth. Our house was always so happy – full of music, dancing, laughing. Now, it's a house of silence, hiding and deep introspection. There are days I don't feel 15 at all. And, the hardest part is I know we are one of the lucky ones in Cuba. We have money, connections, friends and a huge family to support us. What is happening to people without support? Maybe those are the ones that Castro is attracting. He grows more popular and powerful each day in the media.

14 January 1959

The parade was televised as promised. A few neighbors came over to watch because not everyone in our neighborhood has a television set.

Fidel Castro appeared on a truck riding with Che Guevera and Camilo Cienfuegos – two other "heroes" of the

revolution. The truck that was carrying them was also
pulling a trailer full of guerrillas. There must have been
another twenty men on that trailer. The streets were lined
with people yelling what sounded like *"Viva Fidel!"* You
could hear people yelling through bullhorns too.

Castro eventually spoke. It was a message of hate
about Batista and the Guardia Civil that he had supposedly
created to protect the people and instead robbed the people.
Castro spoke about Batista's mob-like rule, what a thief the
man was and how he stole from the Cuban people. Then
Castro switched his speech to what he would do for Cuba.
His message was one of peace, liberty and help for the poor.
The crowd was chanting and cheering for Fidel Castro.

After the neighbors left and we were alone again
Papi told us that a lot of the things Castro said about Batista
were basically true. He was a thief. He did steal from the
Cuban people. But, he also did so much good for the
country. He brought in foreign investors. He built up the
infrastructure – railroads, telephone lines, commercial
airlines, public buildings, etc. He encouraged free
enterprise. He kept the peace, unfortunately, at times with
strong arm tactics. And, he didn't deny people their basic
freedoms and human rights. There was a free press in Cuba,
capitalism was thriving and the country was prosperous.

Papi was extremely worried about the message he
had been hearing from Castro's supporters. It was a
message of distributing wealth – wealth that Papi had
created on his own by building a business from the ground
up at the age of 18. It was a message of anti-Americanism –
Castro constantly referring to the evil *Yanqui* neighbors.
And, Papi was making good business selling to American
companies like Nestlé. It was a message Papi said was
enforced by violence and complete government control.
Plus, the men Fidel Castro had at his side, notably Che

Guevera, came to Cuba with reputations of being assassins and socialists.

Papi did agree with one thing Castro had said in his speech. It was time to move ahead and resume our lives.

18 January 1959

We took J.J. back to boarding school yesterday. Tomorrow we all start back. Papi says that for now the country is quiet and things are moving right along. He says we must all be brave and continue our studies. J.J. seemed okay when we dropped him off at school. Once the fighting subsided and he knew everyone in the family had survived he was much better. Obviously, he has already seen more than Tony and I can even comprehend. He hasn't talked to us at all about witnessing the assassination near the *tostadero*. Like Papi, he's trying to protect us.

I will miss him. We have all gotten much closer. Living in close proximity and enduring the fighting has brought us together as a family. We probably won't see J.J. again until March vacations. For now Papi says we will go to our beach – especially if things continue to remain calm.

I wonder if all of my friends will come back to school now. I hope everyone is fine. I hadn't thought too much about them until the reality of going back to school hit.

Papi says the business survived relatively unscathed. His business partners are all fine which means that Fabuloso is fine. I'm still wearing my locket, but I haven't heard from him since *Noche Buena*.

For a country that survived a revolution and overthrew its government, the changes are not all that evident on the outside.

30 January 1959
The first couple weeks back to school are behind me.
Nothing much has changed. I still like my friends and
dislike my schoolwork.

Now that Papi is back at work full time he has heard
all kinds of rumors about Castro and what happened
immediately after he came down from the Sierra Maestra to
take control of the country. Papi says that so many soldiers
and policeman were killed or assassinated during those two
weeks. He himself witnessed one death.

There are rumors that Castro went into a hospital
that had several injured soldiers from the Guardia Civil
confined to hospital beds. He supposedly went from room
to room killing those men in cold blood. These were men
that were infirm and unable to defend themselves.

Papi says there are people who have "disappeared,"
men that were sent for by Castro's men and never seen
again. He doesn't know what to believe and not believe, but
the rumors are everywhere he says.

12 February 1959
Papi came home today from work very upset. Three men
came to his offices at the *tostadero* and asked to see his books,
his ledgers. Papi says these men identified themselves as
Castro's men. Papi recognized one of the men from Bayamo.
There was also a man from Santiago and one from
Contramaestre.

Papi didn't want any trouble, so he went and got the
books. The men spent hours going through them.
Apparently they brought along black ball point pens and
marked through each page of the ledger by creating huge X
symbols. Papi didn't want to venture a guess as to what it
all means.

Mami is very mad. She says they are sending him a clear message –his business doesn't exist. Papi said they didn't take anything, and thinks she's overreacting. I think the huge X means none of this matters anymore.

16 February 1959

We went up to the *cafetal* this weekend to visit Papi's coffee farm and see Tio Manolo. The farm is fine, and Manolo is healthy. Tio Manolo says that the guerrillas would steal food from time to time, but otherwise they left him alone. Papi wanted to ride out and check the property, and I begged him to let me go. I hadn't been on a horse since before New Year's Day, and I was anxious to ride.

We had a great ride together. Papi and I galloped through the fields, cantered along the fences and let the horses rest near a stream. It was a sunny, mild day. The property was in good shape. And, you could almost forget the last couple of months. Papi looked happy and peaceful. He was on the land he had bought so many years ago and built his business from. I spied him and thought he looked so handsome and heroic. I closed my eyes and rested next to the stream and felt happier than I'd felt in weeks. I didn't want to go back to Bayamo, to school. I wish this moment could have lasted forever.

7 March 1959

Mami and I spent the day shopping. We are going to the beach next weekend. J.J. will meet us there after his midterm exams.

We all needed bathing suits, sandals and some comfortable clothes, so we ended up visiting a few stores. After the second or third store we visited, Mami started to look agitated. Mami told me not to look obvious but to casually look towards the door and check the woman standing there. She asked me if I had noticed the woman standing near the door at another store. The woman in question was wearing a beige suit and had her hair pulled back. I really hadn't noticed her before, but I told Mami there was only one way to figure it out. We had to go to another store and see if we were followed. Mami agreed but she was getting one of her migraines and just wanted to go home. We never did find out if we were being watched all day or not.

On the way home Mami said that the neighbors are falling into two camps. You are either with Castro or against him. She says the neighborhoods, the workplaces, even friends are slowly polarizing. It is becoming dangerous to talk about politics at all.

That night Papi said our family must be like the Swiss. We should avoid discussing anything political or Castro-related at school, work or with friends. He insists we remain neutral.

22 March 1959

We had a great time at the beach! It was so much fun to be together again. J.J. thinks he did well on his exams and seems happier than I've seen him in awhile.

A few of our friends and family came to the beach too. We all stayed at our favorite place, Hotel Lala. Even Fabuloso and family came for dinner one night. They have a house two beaches down from us. Fabuloso looked attractive and tanned, as always. We didn't really get to spend any time on our own. A big group of us ate at the hotel restaurant. There was so much seafood – my favorite. Papi loves seafood too. He ordered some of everything for the tables. Papi always has an appetite. Even during all of the fighting when we were hiding in the back bedroom, he would crawl back and forth from the kitchen to bring us food.

It was a relaxing and enjoyable week. We swam, we sunbathed on the beach, and we played games. Tony dug a hole in the sand and asked me to get in, and then he buried everything but my head. It was like old times for one week.

I was glad to get away from Bayamo for awhile. We all needed the vacation. We will spend Holy Week at home and out of school.

24 March 1959

Castro has taken his assassinations and firing squads public! He is now broadcasting public trials and sentencing from the Sports Palace in La Habana on the radio and television.

Some neighbors came over after dinner to watch the "spectacle" as Mami calls it. She sent us to bed. Mami refuses to watch what is happening and is in the kitchen with her neighbor Mercedes. They have really bonded since Mercedes helped Mami out with the guerrillas. Papi is acting as host in the living room. He doesn't want to particularly watch either, but several neighbors are here. Papi feels obligated to watch.

25 March 1959

I'm glad I was forbidden to watch the executions. I think J.J. came out of his room to watch. Papi says it was a bloodbath. He thinks Castro is just getting started too. Things have been bad all over Oriente where we live. Raul, Fidel's brother, is in command of this province. He is just as bloodthirsty, if not more so, as his brother. If he even suspects that someone is former Guardia or aligned in any way against the revolution, they are on their knees. Papi says there isn't much we can do. We need to be brave, comment on nothing and resume our daily routines.

The papers report that the public overwhelmingly supports Castro and the public executions. There are huge crowds outside the Sports Palace that chant for Castro. Papi says Castro has effectively done away with the judicial system in our country. He says the trials are a joke and that no one with any real legal background is presiding over them. He, like Mami, thinks it has become a spectacle.

29 March 1959

We went to Easter Sunday mass today. The priest, Father Francisco, spoke out against the revolution, Fidel Castro and the public firing squads. He chastised the congregation for watching or listening to the trials – especially during Holy Week. The priest specifically warned Cubans that Castro has a hidden agenda. He put into words the whispers that abound at school and on the streets – talk of Marxism. Father Francisco has heard talk that Castro is only masquerading as a Catholic. He may wear the medal of the Virgen del Cobre (patroness of Cuba) around his neck, but it's not what he carries in his heart.

Only time will tell what Castro's true intentions are, but he's off to a violent start. He speaks of humanism – equal rights for all, universal education and healthcare, an end to poverty, freedom – but he takes human life on national television. Father Francisco ended his homily with a parable, "Beware of wolves in sheep's clothing."

4 April 1959

We went to the club last night for a big dinner honoring distinguished business leaders in Bayamo. Fabuloso was there with his parents. Both Papi and Señor Federico were honored for contributing to the local economy and donating money towards the upkeep and beautification of the public parks. It was a huge banquet with food of all kinds, music and dancing.

Fabuloso asked me to dance several times during the evening. He seemed happy to see the locket he gave me pinned to my dress. I wasn't sure if he would be in attendance, but I'm glad I took extra time to do my hair, apply a little makeup and wear something nice. He was very attentive yet distant.

I asked him what was wrong, and he replied, "I'm ready to leave Cuba, Bella."

"Why?" I wanted to know.

"The political climate is dangerous, and I am more and more unhappy each day in my father's business," he replied. "I think I am making some headway with him. He has not stopped me from applying to medical schools in America and the Dominican Republic."

"Really? Do you think you would leave soon?" I asked.

"I'll be around most of the summer, but if I get my way I'll be in medical school by September," he said.

I was surprised by his conviction. I'm certain he will be gone by September. I'm glad he's been keeping me at arm's length all of these months. I can see now he is completely focused on his career and only amused by me.

8 May 1959

Castro has made another step towards completely controlling the judicial system. Yesterday he announced the suspension of habeas corpus for ninety days. Now he has permission to illegally imprison who he chooses, and they can't do a thing about it. Papi says anyone who opposes Castro can be locked away as a political prisoner. According to Papi, this is another sign that Castro is not living up to his promises and message of humanism.

Papi also says this comes right after a visit from the U.S. Ambassador who wanted to be assured of human rights in Cuba. Papi says that Castro openly detests the Americans and doesn't want any interference from the *Yanqui* neighbors in the North. Castro is slowly isolating Cuba from the United States.

31 May 1959

Yesterday we celebrated Mami's birthday on our cattle ranch outside Bayamo. The farm is on the banks of the Rio Bayamo and is about eleven acres now. Last year Papi sold off most of the land, over one hundred and twenty acres, to a friend of the family. We still have horses, chickens and some cattle. Papi invited everyone in the family. We are also celebrating the end of the school year and that J.J. is back home.

It was a huge party. We roasted several pigs, and we also served *arroz con pollo* and typical dishes. No one was missing from attendance. Tio Miguel is walking so much better now. The cane is gone, and he's hardly limping. Tio Ricardo and Tia Dolores came with the girls. They seem more animated. Tio Ricardo had a joke for me this time. And, I saw Tia Dolores smile a couple of times. She's still smoking, but Mami says that if it helps her then so be it.

The men talked politics for awhile. It was interesting to listen to their thoughts and opinions on what's happening in Cuba. Most of the men are opposed to Castro's handling of the government since he took over. They fear the rumors of Marxism. And, they want the bloodshed to end. Surprisingly, Tio Miguel supports the revolution. He thinks Nando died because of the Guardia not because of the revolution. Papi and others are shocked by his sentiments. In fact, Tio Ricardo is vehemently opposed to Tio Miguel's assessment.

Tio Ricardo said, "Yes. My son died at the hands of the Guardia, but he died because we were under attack by Castro's men. How can you not see that Miguel?"

"You are mistaken Ricardo," said Miguel. "Nando died for pulling some bulls on a country road after dark. That is NOT provocation."

Tio Ricardo replied, "You are missing the point. Before Castro arrived none of that would have been questioned. Bulls would not have been mistaken for weapons. Don't you see that?"

Mami stepped in and said, "I won't have you arguing at my birthday party. Now, enjoy yourselves."

The adults and children played horseshoes, dominos and card games. I had a chance to ride Chocolate after the party ended. It was a great weekend.

14 June 1959

We attended a wedding yesterday in San Salvador. Mami's niece, Magdalena, married Rafael. Rafael renounced his affiliation with Castro and returned home right before Batista left. Rafael went to work at his father's bakery. He looks like he's made a full recovery, and they made a lovely and happy couple.

After the ceremony, there was a small celebration at his parent's home. Mami and Papi gave them an envelope full of cash. Mami says that's what they need most right now. Rafael does not want to attend a university or pursue additional education. They plan to live in Bayamo and possibly open their own bakery one day.

I had never met Rafael before, but he seemed nice and quiet spoken. They look so young, and I guess they are. Mami says they're both 18 years old. Mami was 21 when she married, and Papi was already 27.

22 June 1959

Papi wants to plan a Café Aroma float for this year's carnival. He asked all of us to come to the *tostadero* today. Usually only J.J. goes to the offices to help Papi, so Tony and I are really excited. We haven't been to the *tostadero* in a long time.

The smell is just as I remembered it. It's almost overwhelming – the roasted and ground coffee is so good. It's funny though, I would much rather smell than drink the stuff. Mami and Papi can't begin their day without café. I'm perfectly content to just whiff it for awhile. Ahh!

Mami thinks we're wasting our time. She thinks any kind of celebration will be cancelled this year, but Papi disagrees. He wants to be ready and hope for the best. We look at last year's float and decide to add some color and height but keep the overall basic design. That way Papi hasn't spent too much time or money if the carnival is cancelled.

28 June 1959

It was a smaller celebration than usual, but the carnival happened yesterday. Not as many businesses entered floats. But, there was lots of dancing and eating. Papi's float looked great as always. He recruited some of the worker's children to sit with Tony and me and wave at the crowds. J.J. watched from the crowd. I don't think carnival is his thing. He's still as serious and somber as always, maybe even more so.

Unfortunately, there were lots of Castro supporters at the carnival this year. We could hear lots of political chanting like "*Viva Fidel!*" The five of us stayed out of it as much as possible. There were several children from poorer families that hurled insults at us. They are proud of Castro and what he represents for them. I hate that they are less fortunate than us. But, I know that Papi worked hard for every *peso* he has. And, Papi is always helping out the poor. He treats all of his workers very generously. Mami says he does too much for people. But, he says that he can and that it makes him happy. Papi's generosity must not be the case throughout Cuba. Castro's supporters seem to be growing in numbers according to the papers, radio and television.

12 July 1959

Mami hosted a dinner for Papi's birthday last night at the club. It should have been a wonderful night, but I was sad. Fabuloso has decided. He leaves for Santo Domingo next month to start medical school. I may see him once or twice more before he leaves. He also indicated that his parents are thinking of relocating a lot of their businesses to the Dominican Republic. They fear the rumors about Castro and are starting to make some preparations.

After the party I asked Papi his thoughts on the businesses and Cuba in general. He said, "I don't know what the future holds, but this is my country. This is where I built my business. And, this is where my family came to from Almería, Spain. I have no intentions of leaving."

I'm glad Papi feels so strongly about Cuba. I've never known any other country, and I love it here in Bayamo. I like visiting other cities, but Bayamo is just the right size. All of our family is close by, and I have my school friends too. I can't imagine anything else.

I will miss Fabuloso, and I might never see him again. But, like Mami, I believe everything happens for a reason and eventually works out for the best.

17 July 1959

The news announced that Castro resigned his post as Prime Minister of Cuba! This announcement is so close to the anniversary of when he originally launched his revolution by attacking the Moncada military fortress in Santiago on July 26, 1953. He was imprisoned and then later exiled to Mexico. In December of 1956, he took a boat from Mexico with about eighty five men and landed near the Sierra Maestra, but only a few men survived the attempt to establish themselves in the Sierras, including his brother Raul and Che Guevara. In three years he rebuilt his guerrilla army.

Papi thinks it's some ploy to nullify the upcoming elections. In fact, Papi is convinced Castro is still running the country from behind the scenes. Cuba has had a "puppet" president in place, Manuel Urrutia, who reports to Castro. Papi thinks this is a move on Castro's part to get rid of Urrutia, consolidate his power and declare himself leader – all without holding elections.

We have to wait and see what will happen in the next few days. The country is so fragile right now. It's amazing how much support Castro has among the people.

26 July 1959

Well, Papi was right. Castro was reinstated today just as he predicted. There have been huge demonstrations in the streets of La Habana. The media has been clamoring for Castro to take control. Castro resumed control of the government and said, "It is the will of the people." He says because of the overwhelming support of the people there is no need to hold elections. Castro is once again Prime Minister of Cuba.

The celebrations were broadcast on the television. Again the chanting came across the airwaves, "*Uno, dos, tres y cuatro. Fidel Castro para rato.*" Papi says Fidel Castro is winning people over because he has immense charisma when he speaks. There is a conviction in his eyes and

manner of speech. He had asked the country to decide
whether you are "either for revolution or opposed to it," and
the people have told him where they stand. Like Papi has
said before, this is only the beginning.

4 August 1959

It has been one year since Nando's death. This morning the
family had a memorial service at the mausoleum.

The crowd had considerably thinned out from last
year's funeral. It was mainly the immediate family and a
couple of close friends. Father Francisco said mass for
Nando, and we all prayed. Afterwards, we went to Tio
Ricardo and Tia Dolores's ranch for lunch.

I had just gotten to the point where Nando was not
on my mind daily. I still thought of him, just not as
regularly. Mami says there can be no greater pain than
losing a child. She says it would kill her if one of us died –
literally kill her. I really can't imagine how it must feel. Tio
and Tia seem sad. But, at the same time, they also seem
more at peace. Maybe in a small way they are grateful.
Most likely, Nando would have been forced to join Castro's
army. Papi says it is only a matter of time before Castro
starts a mandatory draft. He is worried about J.J. who will
be 17 this winter.

7 August 1959

Papi has some business in La Habana and has decided to
take us all. Anyway, it is time for Tony to get braces. J.J.
and I have already been through that ordeal with our
orthodontist in La Habana, Doctor Alvarez. Papi has
already booked our suite at the Hotel Lincoln. We almost
always stay there. We plan to take the plane early tomorrow
morning, so I'm trying to get my packing done. The maids

are busy washing clothes, pulling out luggage and getting everything organized.

10 August 1959

It was an uneventful trip up. The city looks just as I left it over a year ago. Not much has changed on the exterior of Cuba since Castro took over. Instead, the changes have been more internal, more covert. You are suspicious of your neighbors and friends. Are they for or against Castro? You hear the rumors. Is Castro just another dictator with different rhetoric? You hear the talk. Why do people just "disappear?" Are they political prisoners? Have they been assassinated?

13 August 1959

Poor Tony! It's his turn to look ridiculous with braces. Mami says it's very expensive to get braces, so it's not very common to have a big silver smile. Tony is miserable. I remember how funny I looked, and how much it hurt when I wore braces. I'm so glad my teeth are straight, and I'm done. Mami says we need to be grateful that we have the opportunity.

I've actually asked Mami to take me to a dermatologist while we are in La Habana. I don't know what's causing my skin to break out. My parents both had clear skin as teenagers. J.J. seems to be fine. But, I now have pimples at 15. I can't stand it!

14 August 1959

The dermatologist said I'm developing acne. It's probably exacerbated by stress and teenage hormones kicking in. He had me sit under a strong sun lamp for thirty minutes. Now my face is all red, and he told me to expect peeling. How dreadful! I also have to start taking a low dosage of antibiotics every day. Why is this happening to me?

17 August 1959

We are back in Bayamo. I overheard the following conversation on the plane ride home between two well dressed businessmen sitting across from me.

The man with the mustache said, "Fidel is trying to get all of the different labor unions to come to the same agreement before the meetings this winter."

The clean shaven man replied, "From what I hear; only the tobacco workers will be a problem. The sugar cane pickers are already on board."

I asked Papi to explain what I'd overheard, and he said, "Castro is trying to consolidate his power. He wants to take over the labor party movement."

"I don't understand," I replied.

"Until now the different groups of workers, whether they are tobacco, sugar, bananas, coffee, etc., have been represented by unions and lawyers that negotiate on their behalf for wages and benefits," said Papi. "Castro will most likely dictate the wages and benefits before too long."

"So what will happen to the workers?" I asked.

"They will get paid what Castro decides. They will effectively lose their voice, their bargaining power with the government, if Castro gets his way," said Papi.

"Will the workers still get paid?" I asked.

Papi said, "Yes. Their wages will be set by Castro. The lawyers and union leaders will have less power."

28 August 1959

We have been invited to attend Fabuloso's going away party at the club. His parents are hosting a dinner tomorrow night. Mami and I spent the day at the stores trying to find something for me to wear. I'm a nervous wreck. I've been biting my nails, and I seem to have sprouted more pimples overnight.

I decided to buy a red dress with white polka dots. I've got red shoes and white gloves to go with the dress. I plan to sleep with big curlers in my hair tonight because I want my hair to look full when I wear it down.

30 August 1959

Well, we've officially said our goodbyes to each other. He promised to write, but I told him not to worry about it. Fabuloso has probably already left the country. And, his parents said they are not far behind him. I don't think I'll ever see him again.

It's funny, but I didn't cry. There have been far too many other things to cry about this year. I think Fabuloso will make an excellent doctor. He is kind, caring and compassionate, and he has the desire. It has been his lifelong dream. I wish him the best. I hope that he is a successful doctor and finds happiness along the way.

8 September 1959

My birthday fell on a Monday this year. I'm 16 now. After dinner, Mami brought out a small cake for the family. No party this year, just a quiet celebration at home. My birthday always signals the start of another school year.

J.J. returns to Camaguey this coming weekend. He has two years left at boarding school. Then he will probably attend university in La Habana. I only have three years to go. Mami kept J.J. home an extra year because he was born premature and sickly. You could never tell now. He's skinny but very tall.

We leave on Friday to take J.J. back to school. We will all go and spend the night and return home in time for Tony and me to start school on the fourteenth.

14 September 1959

Back in school again. I forgot what a drag my studies were, especially the homework. I miss J.J. already. All of the crises we have endured together as brother and sister have made us closer. And, the worse part of starting school again is that I have the hardest teacher at Divina Pastora, Sister Hilda María. She's infamous with the student body.

I've started the year off on a bad foot, too. I thought it would be funny to play a joke on Sister Hilda María. Little did I know that someone had already placed a tack on her chair. She was livid when she sat on it and was out for blood. But, it was too late for me. I couldn't fix what I'd already done. I had reversed my school blazer and had my hair pulled forward in front of my face to make it look like I was sitting backwards. My hair is so long it almost reaches my waist. When she called my name off the roll call list she noticed I wasn't looking at her and yelled, "Daniela turn around! I can't see your face." When I didn't immediately comply she added, "Look at me this instant!"

Everyone was looking at me. I don't know what possessed me, but I responded, "I can see you just fine, Sister Hilda María." Then I flipped my hair back. Well, now I have punishment work on top of my regular homework. I have to copy two pages out of the Bible. The writing is miniscule. It's going to take me all night. And, I think she blames me for the tack too. *Mierda*, boy am I in trouble!

I hope the school doesn't call Mami and Papi. They have enough things on their plate without my sassiness to boot. They have never hit me, but, boy does Mami have a fierce pinch. It's enough to make you yell "Mercy!" What I can't understand is the one time I step out of line I get caught. Tony is always pulling one practical joke or another and hardly ever gets called out on what he's done. I need to find out his secret.

23 September 1959

My friend, Josefa, at school told me her family is socialist. She says they support Castro one hundred percent. I asked her why she's still at Divina Pastora then, and she replied, "The public schools in Bayamo are terrible. My family wants me to get a great education and become a lawyer or doctor."

I responded, "I thought socialists don't practice religion or believe in God."

She said, "You're right. But, what can you do? Once Castro creates a universal education system things will be much better."

"What do you mean?" I asked.

"My father says that Castro's ultimate goal will be to socialize or standardize every school in the country. Every class will teach the same curriculum and doctrine. He says it's only a matter of time. In fact, he's already making overtures to take over the university system," replied Josefa.

"Whatever you say Josefa," I replied. "Besides I don't know of many female doctors or lawyers," I said.

Josefa said, "That is what is great about socialism. They treat men and women as equals. Any job is yours for the taking. Any."

When I got home I asked Papi about what Josefa had said, and he basically agreed with everything Josefa had said about socialism. "Daniela from my understanding, socialists do not believe in God or allow people to worship as they please. And, their main goal is to universalize education, wealth, healthcare, social standing, you name it," said Papi.

"Unfortunately, instead of freeing people, they actually imprison them. Socialists tell you what to study, how much you can eat, what you should do for an occupation, etc. The list goes on and on. They end up dictating every aspect of your life. Worse than that, they control businesses," said Papi.

"What do you mean?" I asked.

"I pray to God that Castro is really not a socialist, but from what I've heard he's just biding his time. What I mean, Daniela, is that he could come in and take Café Aroma and all of the property from us." "Papi, he would never do that," I said. "How could he?" I asked.

"Look at the Russian Revolution of 1917. Read some of the books out there written by Marx and Lenin," said Papi. "Castro has the power to destroy Cuba if he's really a socialist. All we can do is pray and wait. Pray and wait."

19 October 1959

Sister Hilda María is keeping us busy. I hardly have free time, time to think or even time to write. But, I am troubled today. Josefa looked triumphant. She said that according to her father, Castro has authored a revolutionary paper calling for unity among professors, deans and the university system. She knows he will succeed because dissenters are no longer a factor.

I couldn't wait to ask Papi about Josefa's statement. Papi is not aware of any paper, but he says that Castro has probably imprisoned or executed one third of the professors and deans. Papi says that students in general are the most radical and impetuous group in any society. It's a breeding ground for revolution and for dissent. The bulk of the professors who are left probably support Castro. Now, that he is assured a majority of the support, he can control the entire university system.

"What does that buy him?" I asked Papi.

"Castro ensures peace that way – one of the things he promised the people. There won't be any students arguing with his so-called reforms. Plus, he has ultimate say in what is said and done at the university level," said Papi.

21 October 1959

The news today announced that one of Castro's early supporters and leaders, *Comandante* Huber Matos, was arrested in Camaguey by Camilo Cienfuegos, another hero of the revolution. Matos originally sold arms to Castro and led an attack on his behalf during the early days of the revolution. He had recently resigned his post and openly declared that he was for the revolution but not for firing squads and the power plays Castro has been making.

29 October 1959

The news was even more shocking yesterday! Camilo Cienfuegos disappeared in a Cessna 310 outside of La Habana. There is a huge search underway. So far, there is no sign of the plane. The news says that the plane may have been over open water when it disappeared because there have been no reports of crashes in the surrounding countryside.

2 November 1959

Papi just came back from a business trip to Camaguey. He also spent some time with J.J. He says that J.J. is doing well and sends his love to everyone.

Papi said the rumors around Cienfuego's disappearance are rampant in Camaguey. One of his business administrators said that Cienfuegos spent more than a day with Matos before arresting him. They spent the day at Matos' home and were seen talking and having café on the front porch. Matos' wife said she even cooked a big dinner for Cienfuegos, and was shocked when he later arrested her husband.

According to Papi's administrator, Matos shared with Cienfuegos that the main reason he resigned is that he is not a communist, and he fears that is where Castro is headed with the revolutionary government. Cienfuegos also shared his fears with Matos and agreed that he is worried about the direction Castro's policies are headed too. The policies are much different than the ideals Castro shared with him in the Sierra. He went on to say that Che Guevara has swayed Castro. And, he has heard Castro espouse Marxist-Leninist doctrine. All of these rumors came by way of a friend of Matos' wife.

Papi says this is what everyone discusses right now. And, the latest theory on the street is that Castro had Cienfuegos plane blown up over the ocean. Castro wants ultimate power.

But, the media is reporting just the opposite of all of these rumors. The news shows Castro in mourning over the loss of his friend. He still hasn't given up the search. And, he announced that if Cienfuegos is not found, he will declare October 28th a national holiday in his memory.

All of this news has overshadowed a small announcement from the university system. They held elections and essentially consolidated power and control under Castro on October 28th, too. What a coincidence. Or, is it?

4 November 1959
The search has been officially called off for Cienfuegos. Matos is sitting in a jail cell in La Habana awaiting trial. Castro has managed to kill or imprison his opposition. He is

the maximum Prime Minister, and the country must do his bidding.

Papi is taking us to the Sierra Maestra this coming weekend to check on the *cafetal*. It will be nice to get away, even for a few hours. I am sick of school, sick of Castro and sick of everyone taking sides. I wonder how Fabuloso is doing in medical school. I haven't received any letters. I really hadn't expected him to write, but I guess I was secretly hoping.

I need a diversion. Everything has become so political. Even ballet class makes you choose sides. Mami insists I take ballet for my posture and to help correct my scoliosis. Of course, for Mami only the best will do. So, I take classes from a former prima ballerina, Alicia Alonso. I wonder if Mami knows that every time I go to class I have to listen to Señorita Alonso go on and on about how wonderful Castro is for the country and for the people. Maybe I should tell Mami. It might be an escape route from the weekly class.

Cliques have been a part of school since I can remember. The popular girls, the rich girls – only now it's the Fidel girls versus the Castro girls. If you like Castro you call him Fidel. Obviously, you know where I stand. But, I try to follow Papi's example. I am the Swiss girl in a war of insults and conscience.

9 November 1959

We spent a nice weekend on the *cafetal* with Tio Manolo. Everything looks just like we left it the last time. The crops are fine, the fences are in good repair, and the workers appear to be happy. Tio Manolo says there has been talk among the workers about upcoming negotiations with the labor union leaders. Papi is not concerned because he

usually pays more than the minimum requirements. He
wants to keep his employees happy.

I got to ride with Tio and Papi. He keeps a couple of
extra horses on hand because it's easier to maneuver in the
mountains on foot or horseback than by truck sometimes. It
feels great to be in the cooler air. As we were riding Papi
said, "The Sierra Maestra is where coffee beans grow best on
the island. High up above the lush countryside and
beautiful ocean, the cool humid air feeds the plants and
nurtures a growing environment." I thought Papi sounded
so poetic as he talked about what he loves best.

20 November 1959

Castro effectively has control of the Labor Party Movement
governing tobacco, sugar and coffee industries. Now he has
the final word and say on all labor unions. He forced the
movement to bow to his dictates. Castro is still stressing that
Cuba is governed as a democracy, but his social reforms are
not supporting his message. Castro is starting to take
governmental control of all facets of life. He has eliminated
Batista's men, he has taken over the judicial process, he
controls the university system and now he controls the labor
unions. We all wonder what's next.

Josefa at school says that professional associations
and social clubs will soon come under Castro's scrutiny.
She's probably right. He is slowly working his way into
every aspect of our lives. How can people call these reforms
democratic?

4 December 1959

Castro has set the date for Huber Matos' trial. I wonder if he
will televise the spectacle. Our house is becoming the
neighborhood hub for any major announcements because
we have a television set in our living room. They are

expensive and hard to get. Mami ends up having impromptu television watching parties. She has already invited Mercedes over on December 11th, the date of Matos' trial. I hope they show everything.

7 December 1959

Huber Matos will be tried in front of 1,500 people at the Camp Columbia Theater. The trial will be televised. But already the radio and television are filled with reports of his guilt. The media has already convicted him, or is the media working on behalf of Castro? It is reported that the main reason behind Matos' resignation was the appointment of Raul Castro over the armed forces. Now Raul is calling for Matos on his knees so Raul can watch him die. I wonder what will happen to him when he is convicted. Will he be shot? Imprisoned? The wife of Huber Matos has complained openly about his mistreatment. According to her, he is kept almost naked in a tiny cell with hardly any food or water.

15 December 1959

Huber Matos was found guilty on charges of treason by a military panel. He was sentenced to serve twenty two years in prison. Matos testified that he did not have any personal differences with Castro, only ideological ones. He felt the revolution had completely changed in scope once Castro took power. And, he only wished to be released of his duties. His intentions had not been to subvert the government.

Papi says Castro is turning on all of his men of power. Cienfuegos disappeared mysteriously, Matos is in prison, Che Guevara is in North Africa on behalf of Cuba and Raul Castro is not in La Habana but is instead stationed in Oriente province. Castro is more of a dictator than Batista ever was. At least Batista kept a cabinet, ministers, unions, associations, university leadership in place. Castro is governing solo. He has all of the power in Cuba right now, and we, the people, must watch and wait for the next announcement.

On a brighter note, J.J. should finish up his final exams this week and be home for the holidays by the eighteenth. Mami and I have been busy buying gifts, figuring out menus and planning. This year the family did not have its annual reunion in Jiguaní, so *Noche Buena* at our house will take its place. We need to figure out who will make it from Santiago. Mami says we haven't had much to celebrate lately, so she wants to make our party extra special.

19 December 1959

J.J. is home. We are out of school. It's almost *Noche Buena*. And, things have been quiet out of La Habana. You can almost forget that Castro has solidified his position as Prime Minister – a.k.a. Dictator, Supreme Ruler and Tyrant.

Not as many family members as we had hoped are joining us for *Noche Buena*. And, Mami and Papi decided not to invite friends or business acquaintances – just family. The entire Santiago contingency decided to stay home. Tio Manolo is staying in the mountains. Tio Jorge and Tia Celeste are staying in Jiguaní. Really, only the family in Bayamo is coming, and even then it's not everyone. But, we still want to make it as nice as possible.

This year I helped Mami pick out some of the exchange gifts. I had fun shopping in town. The stores are still carrying just about everything they did last year. That's one good sign.

25 December 1959

Mami really worked hard on the party and it showed. We had a beautiful Christmas tree with bubbling oil lights and lots of colorful ornaments. The cook outdid herself with the pork and side items. Mami and I picked out lots of nice gifts for everyone. Papi especially liked his onyx and mother of pearl cuff links. And, everyone was dressed in fun, festive attire. I really liked my red and green plaid skirt and white silk blouse. Mami stole the show in a burgundy, strappy thing that hung great on her curves. I wish I would start developing some curves of my own. I'm 16 and just as stick-thin as ever. Tony still calls me Olive Oyl. The little twerp is just as skinny as I am, but it doesn't matter because he's a boy.

It was fun but also more sober than usual. Normally, by the time we head to midnight mass most of the men are drunk and ready to sleep it off at the church. Last night there wasn't as much drinking, dancing or joking. Everyone was so thankful to be together, to have great food and to be spared the firing squads of the past few months. Every adult knows at least one person who has "disappeared" or died at the hands of Castro's men this past year. The stories tonight kept starting with words like "Did you hear what happened to him? Have you heard what he plans now? And, what's next?"

I'm just grateful to be out of school, with my family and enjoying a *Noche Buena* that doesn't include shots being fired. For all of the reforms and killing that have happened this year, Castro has certainly delivered a sense of national stability.

1 January 1960

It has been one year since Castro swept down from the mountains after Batista's departure. There is no shooting today. We went to the club for dinner but went home before the clock struck midnight. Mami and Papi were tired and not really in the mood to celebrate the New Year. I still miss Fabuloso a bit at times like this during the holidays. I don't really like anyone at school or the club. The only other boy I've ever really noticed was Julian at the Ford agency in Santiago.

It's nice not having to sleep under a bed, in an armoire or in the bathtub to feel secure. It's nice being able to fall asleep in my own bed. It's nice not to be awakened in the middle of the night by the sound of machine gun fire. I can't believe it's been one whole year.

7 January 1960

Our celebration yesterday was very low key for the epiphany. We exchanged gifts, ate well and had a nice day. J.J. has to head back to school this coming weekend and has requested a visit to the Café Aroma warehouse just outside Bayamo tomorrow. Papi says that's a fine idea. We have a lot to celebrate. Papi's business is still intact. We still have our homes and properties.

This past year has been very hard on some of the larger landowners. So much of the properties were broken up as part of Castro's agrarian reforms. He has gained peasant support. The workers that for the longest time worked the land for someone else now have a stake in what they're doing.

We are lucky so far.

8 January 1960

Papi is in his element at the warehouse. He just loves his business and what he does. He knew at an early age that he loved the smell of coffee. As one of ten children, he was expected to help out the family as he entered his teenage years and held down a part time position in a café while still a student in Santiago. By the time he graduated, he was an administrator and had begun saving money to launch his own business. It had always been his dream from as long as he could remember to own a coffee business, so at the age of 20 he moved to Bayamo and set up shop. Papi had been to Bayamo a few times and was really attracted to its smaller size and ripe potential for business.

Now, standing among all that he built, he looked content. He said his favorite sound in the world was the sound of ripe coffee beans mixing, moving, rolling and traveling past each other. Papi said it sounded like "marbles hitting a glass surface."

Tony, J.J. and I headed out back to our favorite swimming pool – the cement enclosed, coffee shells filled dumping area. We dove, jumped and pushed off the high wall into a sea of dark red and brown shells. J.J. and I were getting way too old to be doing this, but we didn't care. It was just too much fun. Besides, Tony needed someone to play with him. It just feels easy to play and act young again, even if it's only for a little while. We are getting exercise, letting off steam and entertaining Tony in the process. Everyone will sleep well tonight.

11 January 1960
Dear Diary,

   We are all back in school and J.J. is gone. My life has returned to some sense of normalcy since Nando's death.

   I'm nearing the end of my notebook, and I'm ready to say goodbye to you. You've helped me deal with death, grief, revolution and huge changes in my life. Thank you from the bottom of my heart.

Yours faithfully,
Daniela

Notebook 2

"*Yo sé que el necio se entierra*
Con gran lujo y con gran llanto, —
Y que no hay fruta en la tierra
Como la del camposanto."
José Martí

(I know when the obstinate are laid to rest
With grand honor and crying,
That there isn't fruit on the earth
Like the fruit of the cemetery.)

6 *August 1960*
Dear Diary,

I couldn't stay away old friend. So much has happened these past few months since I stopped writing. When I was keeping a diary before, it was about death, shooting, changes of government and a polarization among the Cuban people. All of this seemed to be happening around us but never to my immediate family, directly. We were insulated in a glass house watching all of this happen to our neighbors, friends, schoolmates and acquaintances.

Now the tables have turned on us. We are the target now. We are the ones losing what made us Badillas. We are not on stable ground.

Castro has turned the tables on the Cuban people as a whole. Now everyone around us is starting to see him for what he really is and represents.

This morning we gathered at Nando's grave to pay our respects, but we had to do it secretly and without a priest. You see, Castro has decided that there is no God and no religion. The Catholic church is banned from holding services or having schools. Nuns and priests have been put on notice by Castro. They must leave this country or suffer the consequences of defying him. Mami and Papi have decided we will not attend public school this coming year.

Nando's gathering was also a time to say our goodbyes to Tio Miguel and Tia Carolina. They are leaving for America in the next week. They don't want to stay and see what happens next. Their house in La Habana, luckily it's their second home, was confiscated by Castro and given to some Russian dignitaries.

There are so many stories and events I need to tell you, dear diary. The year 1960 started off innocently enough. Castro changed his rhetoric from Humanism to Nationalism. He said it was time to rebuild the Cuban spirit and pride. It was time to take control back from the American Imperialists in the North. Castro nationalized the telephone company which had formerly belonged to an American firm. He put Che Guevara in charge of the banking system. And, he officially abolished separate facilities for blacks and whites. These were all fairly minor changes that were easily accepted by the population.

In early February, Castro invited the Soviet Union to exhibit in a technological and cultural event. The Russians, through their representative Anastas Mikoyan, brokered a deal to send oil to Cuba in exchange for sugar. This deal made President Dwight Eisenhower of the United States nervous. He tried to woo Castro, but Castro was not interested. Again, he fed the people anger and venom about the *Yanqui* imperialists.

On a more personal note, Papi's land in the Sierra was confiscated and reassigned. Papi had thought himself safe, at least for awhile. And, he was spared longer than most. Maybe his bribes of the past slowed the process, maybe his connections and friends helped or maybe it was the distance from La Habana to Bayamo. But, eventually the *cafetal* was reassigned to peasants. At least Tio Manolo was allowed to keep a few acres and the house he had lived in for so long. Luckily, our cattle ranch was small enough that it wasn't touched.

Unfortunately, Tio Miguel and Tia Carolina weren't so lucky. After Castro signed the oil and sugar exchange deal, Russians slowly started to arrive in Cuba. They primarily settled in La Habana and needed houses to stay in and bring their families over to. Castro went straight for the better neighborhoods of La Habana. And, Tio's second home in La Habana was one of the first to go. Thankfully, he's an executive at Bacardí and has a nice relocation package all set up. In fact, it looks like Bacardí is starting to move operations out of Cuba. Tio can't bear the thought of having his house stolen from him and handed over to some Russian. There is nothing he can do, and he wants out.

In early summer is when things really heated up between Cuba and the U.S. The first shipments of crude oil arrived from Russia in June. The main refinery, Texaco, was U.S. owned. Texaco refused to accept and refine the oil. So, on June 29th Castro confiscated the refinery. This was just the beginning. He went on to grab Goodyear and several other huge U.S. companies. Some estimates claim he has taken more than $850 million worth of land and assets from the United States.

In July, President Eisenhower invited Castro to New York for a summit. Castro took him up on the invitation and set up shop at the Thelma Hotel in Harlem where he met with politicians like Gamal Abdel Nasser, Malcolm X and Nikita Krushev. There wasn't a happy outcome for the Americans. Castro did not cease his land grab. He defended his rights to take back Cuba. He came home triumphant and proud of having defended Cuba's nationalism to the *Yanquis*.

The Russians continued to stream into Cuba. Some started to appear in Bayamo. Our house was spared, but on July 28th Castro's men knocked on our door with an order to confiscate Mami's grand piano for some Russians that had moved into a house two streets down from us. Mami was devastated! I think we were all in shock as six men lifted her piano and walked it out our front door. There was nothing we could say or do. We watched from the front window as the men struggled with the piano. Papi had special ordered the Wulitzer for Mami seventeen years ago when J.J. was born. Papi stormed out of the house a few minutes after Castro's men left. Later that night he arrived with one of the Café Aroma trucks and four other men. They had Mami's older piano from the ranch. It was a smaller upright piano, but Mami's face lit up with joy. She gave Papi a huge hug. Then we all joined in on the hug and held each other close for a long time. The heartbeat of our house stopped temporarily, but thankfully the crisis lasted less than five hours.

Another big change affecting Bayamo is a more pervasive presence of Castro's men. Maybe it's a combination of the Russians arriving too. But, it just seems that when you go out on the streets of Bayamo your every move is watched and reported on. There is a more pronounced feeling of spying going on. You no longer know if your neighbors are friends or spies for Castro. Our social structure has literally broken down. Even the club is no longer an oasis of like minded individuals. What was once a refuge has now become a sparring ground of ideology. We are becoming more isolated each day from friends and acquaintances and cling more closely to our family.

15 August 1960

J.J. was harassed today by some of Castro's younger men, boys really. Four soldiers picked him up near the park and told him to get in their jeep and go for a ride. He knew two of the soldiers from his days at Divina Pastora. They were probably two or three years ahead of J.J. in school. Now, they were boy soldiers trying to intimidate him.

J.J. said he would never have gotten into the jeep on his own accord, but the soldiers were persuasive and kept tapping the revolvers on their hips. They insisted they wanted to talk to J.J., and it would be much easier if he just got in. So, that is what he did. J.J. thinks they probably drove around for forty five minutes through the streets of Bayamo.

The soldiers pointed out Papi's stores and the *tostadero*. They drove J.J. by the house. They told J.J. they knew everything about him and our family and that they were watching our every move. They didn't hurt J.J. They were basically playing mind games with him and, ultimately, us, the Badillas.

Papi is upset. He thinks J.J. handled himself well, but he is sorry that J.J. had to go through any of this type of harassment. Mami and Papi are very worried because J.J. will be 18 soon. They don't want him drafted into Castro's army. In fact, they are so worried they have slowly been building a medical case to keep J.J. out for as long as possible. Luckily, he was born premature and had a multitude of problems during his early childhood. Our pediatrician has agreed to "doctor" up J.J.'s file and make him appear much more fragile than he really is, just in case. Papi hopes that it won't be necessary to lie to Castro's army, but he wants to be ready if the need arises. This is all so scary.

28 August 1960

It has been a whole year since Fabuloso left. I hardly think of him now. I can't even remember exactly what he looks like. Papi says his family is now established in Santo Domingo, and he has received the occasional letter from Señor Federico. Apparently, he has offered Papi an opportunity to start a new coffee business in the Dominican Republic. But, Papi is adamant about not leaving Cuba unless he's absolutely forced to leave. He loves our nation too much. Papi was actually conceived on the voyage across the Atlantic. His parents left Almería, Spain in late 1917. It was a long, hard voyage according to the stories his parents told. And, Papi was born in Santiago de Cuba on July 11th. He loves his family very much and is so proud of the

sacrifices they made to give him and his brothers and sisters
a wonderful life here in Cuba. He is too attached to
everyone and the land to just leave without putting up a
fight.

9 September 1960

My birthday celebration was small and quiet. We went to
our cattle ranch and visited with Tio Miguel and family.
Over lunch Tio Miguel says he has changed his opinion of
Castro. He now sees how dangerous and evil Castro can be.
He has been shocked by the land grabbing and policies
toward the Americans. Yes, the poor are seeing some
benefits, but he doesn't agree with the outright stealing of
another man's property. I'm glad that he's come around
now. Of all of our family, he was the only true supporter of
the revolution.

I had a chance to ride Chocolate for a long time. I
actually went out on my own and wandered down toward
the river. I'm glad Papi is still committed to staying in Cuba
despite everything that has happened. I love the island too
much to leave. I love my horse, my life. The list goes on and
on. J.J. and Tony found me down near the water just staring
out into space. We rigged a makeshift swing and decided to
go swimming. It's so nice being a boy. They just stripped
down to their shorts. I had to jump in wearing a jumper.
My clothes kept weighing me down, so I quit swimming
rather quickly. I just sat by the banks and watched them. It
was a peaceful afternoon.

I can't believe school starts next Monday. Or, rather,
it would have started for us next Monday. But, since Castro
cancelled religion for Cuba, Papi has cancelled school for us.
He's not sure what we will do yet. We drove past Divina
Pastora yesterday and it's chained closed. Also, some sicko
took baby Jesus out of the Virgin Mary's arms and replaced

Him with a machine gun. It's behind the locked gate, so no one can replace the gun. But, it's visible enough that everyone can see it.

J.J. is still committed to studying architecture. I'm sure Papi will try to get him into a good university, probably in La Habana. I'm still no closer to knowing what I want to study. My year with Sister Hilda María taught me I have no desire to teach school – not ever! Our class was awful. We played pranks on her constantly. I know that I wouldn't deal very well with the students if I were in her shoes. She's truly a saint.

30 September 1960

Things in Cuba have gone from hot to practically boiling! And, I'm not talking about the temperature. Castro has aligned himself with Krushev, he spoke out against the U. S. at the United Nations General Assembly and defended all of his land grabbing actions and President Eisenhower issued a trade embargo against Cuba. Papi says it's only a matter of time before we start feeling the shortages. For so long Cuba's economy has been driven by trading sugar, beef, tobacco, coffee and cacao beans. He says our economy will suffer, and therefore, we will suffer.

15 October 1960

Castro has implemented a Russian style quota system. Each family in Cuba has been issued a coupon book that they use to receive their monthly rations. Mami has no idea how the average family will survive under this new system. Each family receives a small brown bag with their coupon. The bag usually has two cups of rice, two plantains and one cup of beans. Once a week you must stand in a long line to receive your beef quota, a tiny portion with bones and fat. Then, each family gets a schedule of when they must go to their local store and make any additional purchases. Luckily, one of Mami's brothers, Tio Ernesto, owns a small grocery store. We can always get what we need, but not everyone in Cuba is so lucky.

Since we have our food connection, Mami usually gives our coupons and rations to her niece Magdalena. She and her husband need the extra food since they just married. And, Magdalena is now pregnant.

25 October 1960

Last night the phone rang, and Mami picked it up. It was her Mama Aurora. As soon as she got off the phone she called us all into the dining room. We thought she had some bad news from our grandparents, and we were all anxious. Instead, Mami had a question for us. She asked, "Has anyone heard a small clicking noise before when they talk on the phone?"

"What do you mean?" asked Papi.

"Right after I picked up the phone it took a second or two longer than usual to connect, and I heard these strange clicking noises. I think our phone is bugged," said Mami.

Papi said, "Actually, one of our administrators at work reported the same thing to me yesterday. I wouldn't be surprised at all."

"What do you mean?" I asked.

"Now that Castro essentially owns the telephone company, he can do what he wants, *mija* (my daughter). If he wants to have people listen in on our conversations, it is quite easy for him," he continued.

Mami said, "We must all be careful about what we say on the phone. Most importantly, never complain about the government or Castro. Okay?"

"This is intolerable!" yelled J.J. as he stormed out of the room.

It is really scary how Castro is gaining control of every aspect of our lives. We are suspicious of everything and everyone. Mami says that most of our neighbors have gotten rid of their hired help. Papi thinks it's a great idea. Mami and Papi really only trust one maid. She's an old widow who has been with them since they got married almost twenty years ago. Mami is worried that she will be overwhelmed with the housework and cooking, but there is nothing else she can do. Tomorrow she will have to fire the drivers, housekeepers and laundry help. I guess we will all have to pitch in. I'm not sure what help we can be though. I've never cooked a thing in my life. The least we can all do is pick up after ourselves to make it easier for Mami.

30 October 1960

Magdalena's husband, Rafael, thought he was being followed yesterday from the quota line and came directly to our house. He didn't want to be accused of taking our quota, so he left the brown bag at our house. He pretended he was acting as our delivery boy. He'll be back tomorrow to get the food.

He couldn't have been gone more than ten minutes when there was a knock at our door. One of our neighbors had reported something suspicious to the store owner about the Badilla family. Apparently, she has never seen us go to the quota line, meat store or local grocery for rations. She wanted to know what was happening with our coupons. What she didn't know was that the store owner is our Tio Ernesto who sent someone "friendly" to investigate. That way our neighbor can report back to her committee that her complaint was checked. Tio Ernesto sent us a warning message through his employee to be careful.

Mami has had enough! She strode into the kitchen and filled the brown bag with all kinds of goodies for Magdalena and Rafael. She kept muttering under her breath. She wants so bad to fight what is happening but doesn't want to attract any attention to our family. At least Magdalena and Rafael will get a pleasant surprise in the morning when they retrieve their bag.

Tonight Mami made Papi hide twenty four cans of Spanish olive oil in the backyard. He and J.J. went out after dark and dug some holes. Mami is worried that we may get our house searched because of this nosy neighbor.

2 November 1960

Papi was dejected when he came home from work today. I have never seen him lose his appetite before, but tonight at dinner he kept pushing his food around the plate. He must have been watching the three of us through the years do the same thing on our plate. Mami noticed too and eventually dragged what was wrong out of him.

Castro sent some men to the Café Aroma Warehouse today and "confiscated" some of his equipment. Specifically, the big machine that shells the coffee beans was dismantled. They told Papi the machine is scheduled to be shipped to Russia. Papi could do no more than just watch as the men took the equipment apart piece by piece.

He says he can still manage to run his business with some of the other equipment, but Castro is making it very tough on him. He has to buy more coffee beans than he used to since he lost his *cafetal*. When he makes the purchases, he's not getting good rates. And, now one of his important pieces of machinery is gone. Papi looks so tired tonight. I'm worried about him.

He says the food the cook has prepared is pretty lousy too. That's not helping his appetite. I have to agree.

The one maid that's left is overwhelmed with all of her other tasks.

4 November 1960

Mami must have confided in our neighbor Mercedes because tonight she brought us a scrumptious dinner. Papi was pleased. You see, Mami never learned how to cook. She was one of many girls, and there was always someone around who liked to cook at her house. And, when she married Papi he immediately hired a cook. So, she's helpless in the kitchen. And, I guess I am too.

Papi also talked to Magdalena about our predicament, and she has volunteered to come help out. She is so grateful for all that Mami and Papi have done for them. Papi is happy to have good meals again. And, it will be nice to have another face around the house. It's quiet sometimes without all of the staff.

15 November 1960

It has been strange not having to attend school this fall. Mami and Papi make us read and tell the family about the books we've read, like a book report. Papi keeps our math skills refreshed. He's always been great with numbers and takes pleasure in his books. Mami tries to get us to play the piano, but unfortunately, none of the three of us likes or plays the piano very well. And, the news, or what Castro feeds us by newspaper, radio and television, serves as our social studies class.

J.J. spends a lot of his time drawing and sketching buildings, cars and complex geometric shapes. Tony is always tinkering with the radio, the bicycles – whatever he can get his hands on. I've been reading so much, but now I have to reread some of our books. It's hard to get new books. Papi has some connections. He says the black market is growing in Cuba as shortages become more common. You can still get things in Cuba, but it takes longer and it costs more.

22 November 1960

Some of Castro's comrades came to our door yesterday. There were three of them, and they carried revolvers on their hips. Apparently, they were local soldiers tired of being outside. It is very dry and hot out. It hasn't rained in weeks. I guess the rainy season is officially over. These soldiers told Mami, "We want to rest in Fidel's house for a few minutes and get something to drink."

Mami didn't know how to react. She didn't want anything to happen to us, so she sent us outside to the courtyard in back. Then she told the soldiers, "Come in."

"Comrade Badilla, why don't you make us some of your husband's famous coffee," they asked.

Mami brewed them coffee, they drank it quickly and left the house without much fuss. But, Mami is livid. She feels violated. She doesn't understand how these soldiers can claim our house as Fidel's.

Poor Papi got an earful when he walked in for dinner later on that night. He sympathizes with what Mami went through, but he has seen and been through so much worse. His business is slowly being stolen out from under him bit by bit. His family and friends are leaving the country. And, his children can't even go to school or play outside because they are considered *gusanos* (worms) – wealthy kids who oppose the government.

Mami wants to leave Cuba. She said today was the final indignity. She told us all, "This is not my Cuba anymore. This is not the country where I was born and raised. This is not the country where I want my children to live. We are no longer free here. Castro has made us all his prisoners, his servants." Papi just looked at all of us scanning each one of our faces and didn't say anything. I think his heart is so sad.

1 December 1960

We are all flying to La Habana for the next week. Papi has some business, and Mami wants to take Tony to the orthodontist and me to the dermatologist. My acne is getting worse instead of better. I wash my face religiously and do all of the things the doctor said to do. But, I can't take away hormones or stress.

11 December 1960

Both Mami and Papi were gone a lot while we were in La Habana. On the flight home Papi announced that we will be spending more of our time in La Habana the coming year than in Bayamo. He said there are some tricky negotiations that demand his personal attention. Mami says we will stay at our suite in the Hotel Lincoln as much as possible. Since we are not in school, she said it will be like an extended vacation.

Both of them looked like they were trying to hide something. The three of us kept our mouths shut, but we met in J.J.'s room as soon as we got home. J.J. told us he overheard Mami and Papi talking one night about getting us out of Cuba. He thinks Papi has relented, and they've started the process of getting exit visas. He didn't hear much more than that, but he's convinced that is why we are "vacationing" in La Habana.

24 December 1960

This is supposed to be our first holiday without religion. In effect, Castro has cancelled *Noche Buena, Santi Clos* and *Los Tres Reyes Magos*. Mami refused to listen to Castro's order altogether. She put up a small Christmas tree in the kitchen nestled beside the refrigerator. She even decorated it with a few ornaments.

Tio Ernesto supplied us with a leg of pork. Papi was worried that the smell of roasting pork on *Noche Buena* would alert the neighbors, so he had the leg roasted at the bakery of a friend. We didn't invite anyone over, but the five of us had a nice dinner together and exchanged one gift, our usual custom. Papi got me a copy of *Wuthering Heights*. I don't know how he found it, but I'm grateful to have a new book to read.

After dinner Mami played the piano some. She stayed away from traditional Christmas pieces, again not to attract attention from neighbors, and instead she played her favorite, Chopin. She was inspired, and the music was awesome. Mami easily played for us an hour.

Since we couldn't attend midnight mass, Papi read to us from the bible. It's illegal to own a bible, but everyone I know has kept at least one in the family. We hide ours. I really don't understand how Castro took away religion from the Cuban people. We are overwhelmingly a religious, spiritual and superstitious people. He has taken away part of our identity.

After Papi was done reading to us, he told us he had an announcement to make. They have decided to try to get out of Cuba. Papi says he wants to stay as long as possible, until Castro has taken every last scrap from him. But, he says we can no longer remain in our homeland. That is one of the main reasons for the move to La Habana. He is also worried because J.J. could be conscripted at any moment. His medical excuse is keeping him out for now, but for how long?

I wonder if other families throughout Cuba had similar nights like we did. Did they eat pork, exchange gifts and read from their illegal bibles? Did they set up anti-revolutionary Christmas trees in hidden corners of the house? Do they feel like we do – abandoned, violated, betrayed and angry?

3 January 1961

The news announced today that the United States officially broke all relations with Cuba. Castro is gleeful. Papi says it doesn't matter if relations are officially broken. It's been clear since September where relations were headed. There are more Russians each day in Cuba. Castro has just traded one master for another.

We are still going to try to go to America. We hear good things from our family that has already left. We will apply for political asylum says Papi. Within the week we should be back in La Habana, hopefully, starting the process to emigrate. It's exciting and scary news. We are packing enough for an extended stay. Papi says that when possible we will come back to Bayamo for a week or two, again not to arouse too much suspicion with the neighbors. What a crazy way to live! Afraid of what the neighbors might report back to Castro's men.

8 January 1961

Dear Diary,

I brought you along to La Habana. I feel like there will be so much to write about. My hope is that before we leave Cuba I can hide you in my armoire with the first notebook. We know from our family and friends who have left recently that you can't take very much out of the country.

The Hotel Lincoln is just like we left it a few months ago. There are several families here. We were able to reserve our usual suite on the second floor. The six story hotel is usually a more business oriented hotel, so it's nice to see some teenagers and kids. In the past we always heard English spoken because of the American crowds, but now Spanish is prevalent with a little bit of Russian too. I think Tony will have lots of friends to play with.

It's strange to think back on the past two years since Castro took over. He talked about revolution – ending the corruption, the dictatorship and the poverty in Cuba. Now he is openly Marxist-Leninist. The government is omnipotent, Castro's word is rule and the people of Cuba must stand in long lines for basic staples and food. The only thing Castro has accomplished is to completely ruin this island from coast to coast. Also, a mass exodus has begun. Just about every family staying at the Hotel Lincoln is in our shoes, waiting for permission to leave the country.

15 January 1961

I've made a nice friend in the hotel, Lili. She is a little shorter than me, not quite as skinny but with dark eyes and hair like mine. Her family is from Matanzas. Lili and her younger sister Yoli are waiting to leave Cuba too. We have lots of fun going to the restaurant together. Lili has some family in Miami already that is waiting to take them in and help them get established. We have family in Miami and Elizabeth, New Jersey. I'm not sure where we will end up.

Mami lets us run around alone since we know so many people in the hotel. There are four families from Bayamo – the Espinosas, the Marcanos, the Martinez and the Guerreros. They all have children that range in age from toddler to 18. So, there is always a big group of us together. We hang out in each other's rooms, the halls and the restaurants. Our stay in La Habana really does feel like a mini-vacation. It's hard to believe we might be leaving here soon.

17 January 1961

Tony needed to have his braces checked out, and Mami was reluctant to leave J.J. and me behind. So, the four of us went together. Doctor Alvarez adjusted Tony's braces while J.J. and I waited in the reception area. Tony was only gone a few minutes and returned alone.

I asked, "Where is Mami?"

"She has something to discuss with Doctor Alvarez. She said she would be a few minutes and asked us to wait patiently," replied Tony.

A few minutes turned out to be almost forty five minutes. Mami looked pale when she came out of the office. I asked, "What's wrong Mami?"

"Nothing. Let's go back to the hotel. I'm tired," she replied.

When we got back to the hotel Mami confided that Doctor Alvarez was part of an underground movement to get children out of Cuba. He will be our main contact for procuring our exit visas. Mami says he's helped others get out already and has agreed to help us. Mami says it's only part of the process. Papi has been working to build some connections in La Habana. Doctor Alvarez says it will be a slow process but that we have a good chance of getting out this year.

J.J. wanted to know how Mami knew to speak to Doctor Alvarez. Mami said that on our last visit to La Habana, he had approached her questioning about her intentions. At the time she had respectfully declined and thanked the doctor. Now, things have changed for us, and he is going to do his best. We've known him for at least four years. He has always been very gentle and kind.

I wanted to know why he had not left Cuba. Mami says she had asked him the same thing, and he replied that his wife had never been able to have children. He wanted to help as many patients and children escape before they left. He knew that in Miami his credentials would probably not satisfy the boards, and he would either have to recertify or retire or possibly look for another line of work. For now, he wanted to stay in La Habana as long as possible. Things had not been difficult for him so far. He still had his home, and his life was basically intact.

J.J. was worried that we couldn't trust him. But, Mami knew of several prominent families in Bayamo, Santiago and La Habana that had used Doctor Alvarez's services. In fact, Tio Enrique and Tia Carolina had used him the year before to get their children out first before they left. Mami felt he could be completely trusted. Besides, what choice did we have?

27 January 1961

Mami has disappeared twice this week for three hours at a time. She won't say where she's headed or where she's been when she returns. The only thing she does confide in us is that she's working on our exit paperwork. I think she feels she can protect us if we don't know too much.

Papi has been keeping his regular work schedule here in La Habana. He leaves some time after breakfast and doesn't return to our suite until dinner. We usually go down to the restaurant as a family. For the most part we don't dine alone since we've met so many families on this trip.

Papi doesn't talk much about what has been happening to his business. He has some associates in La Habana, and they have been spending a lot of time together. J.J. has asked to go with him on a few occasions, but so far Papi hasn't allowed it.

10 February 1961

We are going back to Bayamo this weekend. Papi wants to return for a month and check on his business. Mami says she's at a stand still with the exit process. She is still very mysterious about what she's doing. Mami has always been so cautious with us, but now it seems like she leaves us alone for long stretches at a time. I don't know if it's because we're older, because she trusts us more or because she doesn't have any other choice.

I will miss the Hotel Lincoln and my new friends. We've had so much fun this past month. There are so many kids here. Also, most families are staying for the same purpose. They are trying to get out of Cuba and are working on the necessary paperwork. The atmosphere is almost like a party. At home we are so worried about nosy neighbors, quota lines and animosity from people we've known for years. Here, most families have money, are from our social circle and have the same beliefs about Castro. But, it will be nice to see some old friends and, definitely, the extended family.

19 February 1961

We tried to go to the club for dinner, and it was closed. Some time last month Castro's men took over the club. There are to be no more society clubs. In some cities the clubs had to open their doors to everyone. The Club Deportivo was just closed outright. I grew up swimming at the pool, hanging out with my friends in the shade, having dinner in the restaurant with my family and celebrating my debut in the grand salon.

Castro is doing away with all professional associations and private clubs. He's taken away religion. He's stolen our land and redistributed it to people who had no claim to it. He has ultimate control over labor unions and universities. He has made it impossible to attend private schools. He confiscated almost a billion dollars worth of American-owned land and companies. And, he has allied Cuba with communist Russia.

Now, he's driving the Cuban business owner out. Papi is certain his ultimate goal is to control every business on this island. The individual is to be replaced by the government. Papi is finding it harder and harder to do business each day.

21 February 1961

Mami's sister tried to avert a mini-crisis today in our household. It all started with an announcement yesterday that Castro would be visiting Bayamo to give a speech. Each house was ordered to place a small palm tree near the door as a sign of support for the government. In addition, members of the Marxist-Leninist party would be by with signs for each front door that read "This is Fidel's house." Upon hearing the news, Mami decided to openly defy the order.

The hammering could be heard a few doors down. At each house two soldiers were hammering in a nail that would hold the poster with Castro's ownership message. When the soldiers approached our door Mami was there to greet them. She had some tape in her hand. She pointed out the custom woodwork that Papi had special ordered for our front door and requested that the soldiers tape the poster instead of nailing it in. At first they disagreed, but Mami was persistent. She ended up getting her way. As the soldiers were leaving they reminded Mami to place a palm tree at the door.

As soon as the soldiers were out of sight, Mami ripped the poster off the door. She made a show of ripping it up and throwing it out in the garbage can for the entire family to see. A few minutes later, Mami's older sister Eva called to ask if Mami had yet moved a palm tree up front from our courtyard. Mami said, "No. And, I won't. *No me da la gana.*" I could hear Eva pleading with Mami over the phone – to no avail.

Thirty minutes later Mami heard or saw something at the front door that drew her attention. She waited a few minutes and then opened the door. On our stoop was a small can with a shoot from a palm tree. Mami knew who the culprit was. She immediately picked up the can and brought it back to the courtyard and placed it with our other potted palms.

A few minutes after that Tia Eva called again. She told Mami she had happened to be walking by earlier this afternoon and had noticed we were the only house without Castro's ownership sign on the door. Mami very calmly explained to Tia Eva that she had no desire to place such a stupid announcement on her front door. Her exact words were, "Who the hell does Castro think he is? This is my house." We could all hear Tia Eva crying. And Mami yelled out, "*No me importa tres pepinos lo que hacen.*" (It doesn't matter three cucumbers what they do.)

J.J. is the only member of the family who ventured out to Castro's demonstration. He really had nothing to say about the speech afterwards. And, there were no repercussions for Mami's earlier defiance.

24 February 1961

We had a party yesterday at our house for Papa Tato and Mama Aurora's fiftieth wedding anniversary. It was a small gathering because we didn't want to attract attention in Bayamo. We miss the anonymity of La Habana. Here in Bayamo everyone knows us and our family. We had each person bring a dish to share. Before the quotas that would have been unheard of. Mami would have asked the cook to prepare a feast. While we still have enough to eat, it's hard to entertain with what we are given and allowed to buy. Everyone is in the same boat.

Mami and Papi want to get out of Cuba first and then send for Papa Tato and Mama Aurora. Papi's dad is still alive, but he's not in the best of health. He has no desire to leave Cuba. Papi's older sister, Ines, takes care of him at her house. Papi's mom is already buried in the family mausoleum.

Most of the family left behind is starting to talk about leaving soon. Only Tio Miguel and possibly Tio Manolo want to stay. They are older than Mami and have no children of their own. We've already had so many family members leave.

It was easy to keep the party noise level down. Mami had the curtains closed. Most everyone was crowded in the living room and dining room playing dominos, talking or listening to Mami play the piano. We would have normally roasted a pig outside, had a record playing loud and been enjoying the beautiful weather. It makes me feel claustrophobic living like this.

10 March 1961

This is the first time we have not been able to fly to La Habana. Papi said the flights were completely booked. He finds that hard to believe, but he can't do anything about it. I'm secretly looking forward to riding the train. Mami and Papi are not pleased. I think Tony and J.J. are excited too, but none of us wants to let on. We can normally reach La Habana in less than two hours via plane, but the train is going to take at least eight hours, depending on the number of stops it must make.

14 March 1961

We rode a Pullman car on the train. It was very nice and very full of Russians. It was strange listening to their language. It sounds nothing like the Spanish language. Their speech pattern sounds short and clipped. Whereas, most Spanish speakers sound like they are almost singing. There's a rhythm to our speech.

Most of the Russian men wear their hair cut very short, like a military cut. Papi is taller than most of the men. The Russians do not smile. It is so different than what we are used to. Cubans smile at each other, even if they don't recognize the person across from them. The Russians look right through you. They also drink quite a bit. Papi did not allow us to go to the dining car. He brought us snacks and made us stay in our car except to go to the bathroom.

I still had fun. It was a new experience. Plus, the motion of the train put Tony right to sleep. That made the ride more enjoyable. Mami and Papi were grateful that it was a quiet trip. J.J. asked Mami if he could go with her sometimes on her quest to get us out of Cuba. She said that Papi and she will have to discuss it when they get some time alone. I didn't even bother to ask. Papi is increasingly protective of me these days. I know what the answer will be.

17 March 1961

Two of Tony's friends have their exit visas. They leave in a week. Tony will be sad to see them go. Mami takes it as a good sign that they are getting out of Cuba in the near future. That means there's hope that our turn is coming soon enough.

Papi says the communists are just as corrupt as the members of the Batista regime. To get anything accomplished in the new government requires as much *mordida* as in the past. Papi has been bribing a communist friend and connection. He says that next week Mami has to go meet an intermediary for the next step in the process. Between Doctor Alvarez and Papi's connection, they have procured an interview for Mami to plead her case. Papi thinks it would be a good idea for J.J. to accompany her. Papi wants me to be in charge of Tony while Mami and J.J. are gone.

20 March 1961

Mami took J.J. with her today to Doctor Alvarez's office. J.J. said they waited in the reception area until their names were called. Then the secretary, one of the coordinators of the underground railroad, took them back to an examination room and shut the door. From there, they went through what appeared to be a closet into a passageway lined with books that connected to a smaller office. Doctor Alvarez joined them within minutes. He told them that he had scheduled a meeting for them tomorrow at the main office where they process the exit visas.

Doctor Alvarez said that tomorrow morning we should take a taxi or bus to the main reservation office of Iberia Air Lines in La Habana Vieja (Old Havana). Iberia is the main carrier for flights between Cuba and Spain. They are located roughly in front of the Catedral de la Habana, the second oldest cathedral in the New World. The doctor went on to say, "Make sure that the taxi or bus does not drop you off too close to the offices. You must walk a block or two." There were more instructions, but J.J. wouldn't share them.

I really wanted to go, but Mami was adamant that I had to take good care of Tony while she and J.J. were out on this mission. She said I must think of the entire family. Also, she is trying to get visas for her sister's two children. And, Doctor Alvarez wants her to help others too. Mami agreed to take J.J. once to appease his curiosity and Papi's nervousness. After that she intends to handle this on her own.

21 March 1961

I had a lousy time watching Tony today. He kept asking me questions, pestering me to play with him and dragging me up and down the hotel. Mami and J.J. were gone for three long hours. Mami could tell I was very upset about being left out and put in charge. Also, it was pretty clear she had a migraine. Tony begged Mami to let him go down the hall to play with some friends, so Mami readily agreed. When Tony left, Mami swore me to secrecy and told J.J. he could tell me the details of their appointment. J.J. made it sound like a spy mission. I'm so jealous!

"We took a taxi to La Habana Vieja and had the driver drop us off at a park a few blocks away from the Iberia offices. We took an indirect route and eventually found our way to the place. Mami asked some questions at the main counter and then asked where the restrooms were located. She thanked the lady behind the counter and said she would be back for more information. Mami had already been told to find a specific restroom on the second floor, but she asked anyway. From Doctor Alvarez's instructions, it was pretty easy to find. The small bathroom was completely paneled in wood. You had to look closely, but eventually you could make out a door hidden by the tongue and groove paneling. We squeezed through a very narrow door and closed it behind us. A long flight of wooden stairs – poorly lit and narrow – led us to one of the offices of the underground movement.

"There was one man in the office. He was young, probably a university student, pale and chubby. The room was probably smaller than your bedroom at home with only the one entrance from where we came. I was feeling claustrophobic because the poor person didn't even have a window. And, it was just as dark as the narrow stairs. He didn't seem to mind and appeared to be extremely busy at his desk. It was obvious the fellow was not much older than me, but Mami called him Señor and asked him for help. He wasn't overly friendly. Maybe he's just a silent, serious guy. Anyway, he asked Mami how many forms she needed and gave her some sheets to fill out.

"I'm not sure what was on the forms because the man asked for my help. The overhead lights had burned out and he was working from lamp light. He wanted me to keep his rotating chair steady while he changed the bulbs. That took awhile. Then he asked me to help him file some of his cases in alphabetical order. Behind his desk he had a wall of shelving. The last names of each applicant were written on the outside of the manila folder. He had a stack of twenty to thirty cases that needed to be filed. He had other odd jobs that kept me busy while Mami wrote. We were probably in the small office for over an hour.

"We rode a bus on the way back to the hotel. The bus didn't take us directly here, so we walked a bit past the few shops that are still open. We took our time, took in the sights and actually walked past the hotel first. I'm not sure we needed to take so many precautions, but Mami wanted to appear nonchalant. If we were followed, I never noticed," said J.J.

"When does Mami go back?" I asked.

"I'm not sure. The clerk indicated that it may take some time to get all the paperwork, permits and visas done," said J.J.

"I wish I could have gone," I replied.

J.J. said, "Mami doesn't want to take me again. It's much easier for her to move around and blend in without me. Besides, I ended up helping the clerk out almost the entire time."

I was still jealous that I hadn't been invited along. The boys always get to do cool things. I'm always chaperoned and watched closely by everyone. Mami says it's the curse of being a Catholic, Cuban female.

31 March 1961

Today is Good Friday. This is the first time we haven't celebrated *Semana Santa* (Holy Week) since I was born. You can't even go to church today. At least it's raining, though. Mami likes it when it's dark and ominous on the anniversary of the day Jesus died. Some of the women are meeting in a room down the hall to say the rosary. Mami has invited me. It's nice to be included with all of the adults.

I don't know what we'll do for Easter Sunday. Normally we would attend mass and then have lots of family and friends over for lunch. I know we'll still have the lunch part in the restaurant. The waiter, Eduardo, has already reserved a room for the few remaining families from Bayamo. He knows us all by name and really takes good care of us. His sister runs the beauty parlor in the hotel. Mami goes there frequently. She offered to have my haircut done here, but I think I'll wait until we get back to Bayamo. I've been going to the same lady, Margarita, since I was born. She's never given me a bad haircut.

10 April 1961

Tony really did have an orthodontist appointment today with Doctor Alvarez, so we went. When we got to the reception room there were two Castro army soldiers waiting in the office. Mami looked like she was about to faint. She got deathly pale. I held her under the arm and took her to a seat. The receptionist called for Tony a little while later, and we all went in. Mami was concerned that we looked too suspicious, but Doctor Alvarez said not to worry so much. He said Tony legitimately had braces on. He also told us this was not the first time soldiers had sat in the waiting room. But, he was unconcerned. There was absolutely nothing kept in the office that could tie him to the underground railroad. Also, the same thing was going on at other doctors' offices. The doctor adjusted Tony's braces in a few minutes, and we quickly left for the hotel.

Poor Mami is a nervous wreck since she started this whole process. She's been getting her migraines with more frequency. And, she appears skittish all of the time. Mami constantly looks over her shoulder. I told Papi about my observations, and he told me not to worry. They were both doing what they felt was necessary for their children.

17 April 1961

There are so many rumors flying through La Habana. People are talking about an American attack with planes. There is talk that Cuban exiles landed at Playa Girón. I asked Papi where that was, and he told me it's southeast of La Habana facing the Isla de la Juventud (Isle of Youth) near the Zapata Swamp. It faces the Bahía de Cochinos (Bay of Pigs). The news is not reporting anything unusual. But, everyone is talking about the Ataque a la Playa Girón where at least one thousand exiles landed on the beaches in hopes of fighting against Castro's regime.

One of Papi's business associates here in La Habana said that everyone who is opposed to Castro is ready to join the rebellion if it is successful. Castro has confiscated all guns throughout the country, but people have shovels, pick axes and machetes, anything they can use as weapons, placed near their front doors.

I remember when Castro's men started confiscating guns. Papi was reluctant to turn in all of his guns. He was wondering how he would defend his family if someone threatened us. I actually showed Papi how I had loosened the base panel in the bottom of my armoire to hide my diary. Later that evening I heard Papi working in his armoire. I know that Papi hid his favorite gun, a Smith & Wesson .38 caliber revolver, that night. It's our little secret.

I'm sure he wishes he had his gun with him right now. I've never shot a gun, but I wish I had something in my hands right now I could use as a weapon. There must be something to this invasion if the news is keeping it completely silent. What is even more interesting is that Castro officially declared just yesterday he *is* a socialist. Those two things must be connected.

20 April 1961

There is finally media coverage about the invasion in the Bahía de Cochinos. The news is now reporting a crushing victory against American trained Cuban exile forces. Most of the exiles were captured before they could make it out of the Zapata Swamp. The television and radio coverage says Castro has taken hundreds of prisoners. I wonder if we have any friends or family that participated in the attack.

According to the media, Castro plans to hold the prisoners hostage until the Americans trade them for money. He is demanding over fifty million in ransom for the exiles. This reaffirms Castro's rhetoric regarding the *Yanqui* slave masters of the north. He is enjoying the moment completely – gloating over the victory, laughing at the exile rebellion that was completely repelled in three days, showing just how "evil" America truly is and rallying the population behind his revolution. If only he realized people were so willing to take arms against him. If only he knew how much we want to leave our island for the promise of freedom ninety miles to the north. If only the invaders had been successful…

25 April 1961

Mami says our liaison at the Iberia office is unsure of how long it will take to obtain our exit visas because of the invasion. Some of his contacts within the government are a bit jumpy right now. Usually they are easily bribed, but now they are reluctant. He suggested we try back in a few weeks for an update. Mami and Papi are sick of living at the hotel. They want to be back at home to see their family and to tend to what is left of their business and properties.

Mami's birthday is approaching in May. So, the plan right now is to fly home in a few days and return in June to check on the progress of the exit visas. I'm glad we are going home. It's great fun in the hotel, but I miss Bayamo. I hope this won't be the last time I get to see home. It's so strange to think that Cuba won't be our home for much longer if everything goes as planned.

Mami is still clinging to the hope that we can leave Cuba before the year is out. The report she hears from her family in the United States is very positive. More than anything, Mami and Papi want us to grow up free. Batista might have been corrupt, but we had freedom and prosperity under his government. In fact, in 1958 Cuba exported more beef than any other country in Latin America. Castro has completely taken away our freedoms – press, speech, religion, right to bear arms and business ownership. He has left us with nothing and destroyed our economic system.

8 May 1961

We've been home for over a week. Magdalena had her baby, a little girl, and named her Silvia Isabela after her mother and my mother. The baby is adorable. Mami would have been the godmother, but now all religious ceremonies are banned. Mami had some holy water from the church, so she used a few drops to sprinkle on the baby's head and said a prayer. It's the best she can do in a crisis. Magdalena wants to keep cooking for us, but Mami won't allow it.

Papi volunteered to help out with the cooking since he doesn't work as long. He's trying to keep things going, but the communists are confiscating his machinery piece by piece. A few *cafeteras* have been taken over too. Papi is just waiting for them to take everything right out from under him. The one or two times Papi has cooked before, everything was drenched in olive oil. Papi thinks that olive oil helps with joints, muscles and cures all ailments. At least he cooks. Mami can't seem to even boil water.

12 May 1961

Mami thinks that neighbors are spying on us. She has started to close the curtains as soon as it gets dark. We've been eating in the kitchen at the smaller table instead of the dining room. She doesn't want anyone reporting back to the communists that we still have food. And, yesterday, while Tony and I were out back, we could have sworn we saw two heads peering into our courtyard over the stone and stucco wall. We had been outside for awhile when I had a strange sensation like someone was staring at me. I turned around quickly and saw what appeared to be two heads duck down from behind the wall. I could be wrong, but it was such a weird feeling.

Mami's good friend, Mercedes, says she's convinced the lady three doors down is a communist. Mercedes has heard other neighbors report that this lady, Juana, has a son in Castro's army and was an active supporter of the revolution. Mercedes thinks that Juana is the appointed leader of our neighborhood spy ring. According to Mercedes, every neighborhood has an assigned leader that reports any suspicious activities back to the main communist party office in each city and town.

Mami is furious and nervous. Papi says there are spies everywhere and that we need to be extremely careful. He says if any friends or neighbors bring up the subject of politics, we need to remain neutral. He says it's very important that we not lose our heads and get into any heated discussions that might implicate us in any way.

Although the firing squads are not as prevalent as they were in 1959 and 1960, we still need to be careful. Raul Castro is a vicious enforcer. And, one of the rumors Papi hears on a regular basis is that Che Guevara plays Russian roulette every night in the prison when he's bored. Papi told me it's a game where the revolver is empty except for one chamber – one bullet. Che spins the cylinder and pulls the trigger. Sometimes the prisoners are spared, and sometimes Che gets a kick killing an unlucky soul. The last thing our family needs is for any one of us to be imprisoned before leaving. Papi says that prisoners are tortured, kept in tiny cells with only a bare minimum of food to survive and subjected to the whims of the soldiers.

I don't understand how this can be happening to such a sunny, happy island and people. We are the land of the Cha Cha Cha, Rumba and Mambo. We are the land that produced incredible musical genius like Ernesto Lecuona, Desi Arnaz, Xavier Cougat and Celia Cruz. We are the land of beautiful casinos. We are the land of kilometers and kilometers of gorgeous coastline. We were the playground of the rich and famous. Up until 1958, Cuba was called *La*

Perla del Caribe (the Pearl of the Caribbean). Now we are a dark, twisted and subjugated nation.

27 May 1961

We had a small celebration for Mami's birthday. Several family members drove to Tio Jorge and Tia Celeste's farm in Jiguaní. Papi took great pleasure in the forty five minute drive. He has decided to sell his latest Oldsmobile. From now on we will have to walk, take taxis or ride the bus. Our driver was let go long ago. At one point, Mami and Papi probably had eight people on staff. Now we have the one maid, Aurelia, the one that Mami had known the longest and believes to be loyal to us over the revolution.

The size of our extended family here is dwindling. Papi says it's a great sign. I get scared when I think about mastering a new language and trying to fit into a new society. If Mami and Papi are worried, they don't show it. They are fully convinced it is what they must do to protect their children.

Tia Celeste made Mami a beautiful shawl. She knit it with black and white yarn. Mami loves it because she can drape it over her shoulders to shield her from the sun. Light skin is a status symbol for society women in Cuba. The darker the tan, the more you work outside. It is unseemly for a lady of high social standing to work in the yard or stay in the sun so long as to acquire a tan. Mami is proud of her white creamy skin. She has taken to wearing long sleeves even in the extreme summer heat.

31 May 1961

Castro has taken another step toward setting up a totalitarian regime. He has rejected the Constitution of 1940 and cancelled elections. Papi has read a lot about Russian history and says that Castro has set himself up like Stalin, one of the most infamous dictators known for his brutality. If anything gets in Castro's way, he crushes it. He executes anyone in opposition to his policies. Castro has no regard for our basic liberties. He truly is a wolf in sheep's clothing. He has deceived the middle class, consolidated their support and then has taken away their civil liberties, livelihood and "Cubanismo."

4 June 1961

We are on our way back to La Habana again. Mami has agreed to get Nando's surviving sisters out of Cuba for her sister Tia Dolores. The girls will go over first, and then Tio Ricardo and Tia Dolores hope to follow immediately after. Mami is ready to resume the process for herself and for her sister. I already miss our home. As much as I like the atmosphere and friends at Hotel Lincoln, I would rather sleep in my own bed and be in our house.

9 June 1961

There is a younger, newlywed couple staying in the hotel. They are friends of Magdalena and Rafael. They are originally from San Luis, a small town near Santiago. Like Rafael, the man, José Manuel, served with Castro briefly in the Sierra. He witnessed the bullet Rafael took for stealing a can of condensed milk and snuck away as soon as he could. José Manuel and his wife, Luisa, are eager to go to the United States. They asked Mami and Papi for help. Mami agreed to take them with her Monday to the offices of Iberia. Papi told them to be extra careful.

12 June 1961

Mami came back from her visit to the Iberia offices shaking like a leaf. I've never seen her so agitated in my entire life! She thinks they were followed when they left the building.

Mami said she followed her routine of walking a few blocks
before hailing a taxi. As they were walking along La
Habana Vieja they passed a jeep with four soldiers. One of
the soldiers looked long and hard at José Manuel. They
quickly found a taxi and started back towards the hotel. José
Manuel noticed the jeep was following them.

Mami got nervous and had the driver drop her off in
front of a clothing store. She thinks she spent thirty minutes
inside looking primarily at olive green dresses. Mami says
that's the only color readily available in La Habana – maybe
it's the only color they make in Russia. She eventually
walked back to the hotel and circled it once before entering.
There was no sign of the jeep. She is anxious to find out
what happened to Luisa and José Manuel.

13 June 1961
We've been waiting all day to hear from Luisa and José
Manuel. They haven't been seen at the restaurant. Mami
called the front desk in the late afternoon to ask for their
room, and the receptionist said they had checked out. Mami
doesn't know if they got nervous and left La Habana or if
they were picked up by the soldiers. She's going to give it
one more day and then visit Doctor Alvarez.

15 June 1961
Doctor Alvarez hasn't heard anything about the office at
Iberia being discovered. But, just in case the soldiers in the
jeep followed Mami to the hotel, Doctor Alvarez thinks we
should leave La Habana for a month. It's just a precaution.
He thinks that if the soldiers had something on the office,
they would immediately shut it down. He wants Mami to
be safe and sound.

Papi agrees, so we are leaving the day after
tomorrow for Bayamo. That was the first flight he could

book. I'm worried about Mami. She jumps at the slightest noise and is constantly looking behind her wherever we go. Mami is very jumpy. Papi says it will do her good to be around her family again. Also, Papi wants Mami to devote time to the piano because it always calms her nerves.

20 June 1961
Mami rang up Magdalena and asked her to come over for coffee. Magdalena came right away and brought baby Silvia with her. She has grown so much in a couple of months! Magdalena hasn't heard anything about Luisa and José Manuel. But, she will see if Rafael knows of their whereabouts.

It's so nice to be home again. I don't realize how much I miss Bayamo until I come back. I will miss the food at the Hotel Lincoln. It looks like we are going to have to get use to Papi's cooking again – everything drenched in olive oil. Mami insists that Magdalena needs to stay home with the baby. Rafael has been using our quota coupons while we've been gone, but he hasn't had Mami's supplements in awhile. So, Mami went to the kitchen and gave Magdalena what she could find, which wasn't much. Tomorrow she and Papi will go visit Tio Ernesto's store and buy supplies.

Papi says this back and forth between La Habana and Bayamo is good. It keeps the neighborhood spy committee on its toes. Papi is eager to visit what is left of the businesses tomorrow. He has agreed to bring us all along if we want. I can't wait to drive through the streets of Bayamo. It really is a beautiful city. La Habana is too big and imposing for me. I like that La Habana is near the water. But, I love being able to see the mountains and the river in my home town.

I hope that the United States is as beautiful as Cuba. I will really miss our coconut grove the most. We have at least an acre or two planted solid with coconuts at the ranch. I love sipping the coconut milk. Do they have coconut trees in Miami? Mami says they must because it's only ninety miles north of Cuba and just as warm. She's pretty sure if we end up in Elizabeth, New Jersey it will be a huge change for us. They have real winters with snow and freezing temperatures. I've never had to wear anything more than a sweater in my whole life. It would be an adjustment for all of us.

22 June 1961

Papi's café business is barely hanging on. His supply of coffee beans is dwindling. He has had to return to antiquated ways of shelling and roasting the coffee beans since his equipment was sent to Russia. And, Castro is demanding that Papi close all of his cafés. He also had to reduce his workforce considerably. Mainly family is left now in the offices. They are loyal to Papi. They know that we are hoping to leave Cuba soon. Some have made arrangements to leave too, and others are not sure of their future plans.

We took a taxi today. I miss our car. Papi misses driving. He mainly employed the driver for Mami because he always enjoyed being behind the wheel. On the way home I convinced Papi to ask the taxi driver to go by the club just to take a peek. I miss our old hangout. Boy were we shocked when the town looney, Matilde, was hanging out by the pool. Papi decided we should get out of the taxi and walk around. Papi says he gives Matilde money whenever he sees her on the street and feels a bit responsible for her. She has always been a bit crazy.

Papi approached her and asked about her health and well being. Matilde said, "Oh, I'm just fine. I'm enjoying myself by the pool. You know they always turned me away from this club. But, for the last couple months I come out here and swim, sun myself and walk along the grounds."

Papi replied, "Doña Matilde, this water hasn't been cleaned in months. It is probably very dangerous for you to swim here. You see, the club was closed."

"Now don't spoil my fun. I just love it out here. Nobody messes with me," said Matilde.

"Do you need any food or money?" asked Papi.

"No, I'm just fine. Thank you for asking, though," she said. "I've never eaten better. The kitchen pantries here are stocked with rice, beans and pasta."

"Well, good day. Take care of yourself," said Papi.

As we walked back to the taxi I asked Papi if he didn't think her behavior was weird. Papi says Matilde has always lived in her own world. She sort of lives with her brother, but she prefers to be out on the streets. Papi says most towns have one or two individuals that are a bit crazy. Papi thinks she's currently having the time of her life inside her head. In her mind, she has officially been admitted into one of the most exclusive clubs in Bayamo.

Mami enjoyed our story about Doña Matilde even though she feels sorry for the poor lady. She stayed home today because of her migraine, but she was feeling better when we got home. Papi persuaded her to play the piano while he cooked. It was a nice evening. We all commented on how we missed our waiter Eduardo from the restaurant. The Hotel Lincoln really has become our second home.

4 July 1961

Tio Ricardo was almost arrested today! Apparently, today was his day to purchase beef at the butcher's shop. He got to the shop late because one of his daughters was up vomiting all night with a stomach virus. He must have slept

in. The lines are worse the later you wait to make them.
Anyway, he says he patiently stood in line for two hours
before it was finally his turn at the counter. The butcher
handed him a tiny package, and Tio Ricardo opened it up
right there. He was appalled when he discovered it was full
of bones and fat – no meat at all.

Our neighbor Mercedes was in the shop in line a few
places behind Ricardo. She said all of a sudden he started
screaming at the butcher. He threw the package down with
disgust and yelled some obscenities. Mercedes recognized
him and forcibly dragged him out of the shop because the
butcher was threatening to call the police. She brought him
over to our house.

Mami was so grateful to Mercedes and so mad at
Ricardo. She yelled at him for being irresponsible. She
reminded him that he still has daughters on the island and a
wife. What would they do without him? Ricardo was
subdued. Mami went back to the kitchen and came out with
food for both of them. We had just received some groceries
from Tio Ernesto, so our pantry was full. I was proud of
Mami. She handled the situation well and seems stronger
since we got back to Bayamo.

12 July 1961

Che Guevara spoke today. In his speech he praised the
Russian women he has met. They are some of the sturdiest,
strongest comrades he has ever known. He says it is time for
the Cuban women to toughen up. Russian women do not
get aches and pains like their Cuban sisters. From now on,
Cuban women will no longer get aches and pains either.
Che has taken aspirins off the pharmacy shelves. Mami is
not surprised. She says the supplies at the drug stores have
slowly been dwindling. She laughed at Che's speech. She

said it's just propaganda to cover up the fact that Cuba is running out of medicines.

Papi is very worried about Mami's migraines. Mami is not too concerned. For now she has her stockpile. It should last her through the month. She hopes that by August some medicines will be available. Maybe we will have sold the Russians more sugar by then to be able to afford basic human necessities. What a pathetic existence! This is yet one more example of how Castro and communism have failed Cuba.

17 July 1961

Magdalena and Rafael have not been able to track down Luisa and José Manuel. It's unnerving not knowing what happened to them that day on the street. Did the army jeep stop their taxi? Did they lose the soldiers following them? Are they hiding out somewhere? Mami and Papi have decided we have to chance it and return to La Habana. There is no time to lose. We must put our trust in God, and we must leave Cuba as soon as possible.

Mami wants to leave this coming Sunday. Papi says let's just go tomorrow. Why wait? But, Mami is adamant. She says she has some shopping to do. She wants to see her family. And, she wants us to go to Tío Ricardo and Tía Dolores's farm one last time. Tony is excited about visiting them again. They took our pets in when we started to travel between Bayamo and La Habana with some frequency. Tony can't wait to see Terri Tambien and Paton. I wish I could see Chocolate one more time. Tío Miguel is still overseeing our animals and grounds. Luckily, the communists haven't taken our ranch away yet.

23 July 1961

Surprise! Mami managed to surprise us all. She must have
been working for a week or two with Tio Ricardo and Tio
Miguel. It was Papi's birthday two weeks ago, and we cut
our customary cake and exchanged a few gifts alone at
home. Before Castro, we would usually host a huge dinner
at the club in Papi's honor. Mami must have decided Papi
would still get his big dinner. So, Mami got all of our family
to come to Tio Ricardo's ranch and surprise Papi. Mami
managed not to let any of the three of us in on the secret, so
we were all ambushed together. It was great!

Mami must have read my mind, too. Or, maybe I
said something and don't remember. But, Tio Miguel led
Chocolate out to me with a huge smile on his face. He
confessed to trailering the horse for the short ride over
because he knew I would want one last ride. Papi took
mercy on me and told me to go. Paton was busy licking J.J.'s
face, and Tony was already leading Terri Tambien by a rope.
I didn't realize until this moment how much we missed our
pets. I could feel the tears coming, so I got up on Chocolate
as fast I could and rode away.

The tears were coming faster and harder now. The
enormity of leaving Cuba finally hit me today. Up until
now, it had been a game – going back and forth between the
hotel, visiting Doctor Alvarez's office, watching Mami
disappear for two or three hours, wondering how much
money Papi was paying out to make this happen – all a
game. Now the game was almost over. God willing, we
would get our exit visas soon. My heart aches so much
when I think about leaving my home, my cousins and
family, my parents temporarily, my home town and my
animals, my country and my café cubano.

I'm actually writing this on the plane back to La
Habana. As scheduled, we still left on Sunday. Papi is

happy that Mami insisted we stay in town longer. It was good for the entire family to spend time with each other. Papi wants us to leave with happy memories of our childhood in Cuba. He worked so hard and built his businesses up from scratch so that his children could enjoy the fruits of his labor.

Last night when we got home from the surprise party Papi said, "Castro has taken so much from the Cuban people physically and emotionally. But what I find saddest of all is that he has taken away people's hope. Cuba was a land of opportunity. I am an example of what you could accomplish. I started at 20 years of age with literally nothing – just the little money I had managed to save from a part time job, and I built a very successful business. Before Castro, anyone had the opportunity to make something of themselves if they worked hard. Now, Castro has in effect created a welfare state where every citizen waits for his/her monthly allotment of food and money. There is no opportunity to better your lot in life. He has taken away our hope. I want hope for you children. I want freedom. We can no longer live here with our spirits imprisoned. I will miss Cuba more than you can imagine, but we have no choice."

24 July 1961

We are at the Hotel Bristol. Our suite at the Hotel Lincoln was not available. It is reserved until the sixth of August. Papi went ahead and paid the manager at the Hotel Lincoln for August and September so that we can stay there as soon as the other guests leave. The Hotel Bristol is a fine hotel, but they don't have suites. We had to get adjoining rooms. Mami is not happy, but at least it's only for two weeks. We don't know if there are any families from Bayamo staying here. Also, Mami hates going to new restaurants with us.

The three of us are all picky eaters. We have gotten much better since the food quota system started. The three of us are really trying to make this whole process easier on Mami and Papi. They look drained.

26 July 1961

Today is the anniversary of Castro's revolution. There were huge crowds in the street. You could hear the familiar chant, "*Uno, dos, tres y cuatro. Fidel Castro para rato.*" But, there was another chant, another voice behind the crowds that said, "*Uno, dos, tres y cuatro. Comiendo mierda y rompiendo zapato.*" Eating shit and breaking shoes! I love it. There is probably no worse insult to the Cuban people than calling someone a *comemierda* – shit eater. From the sounds of the crowd, some of the people think Castro is the consummate *comemierda*. I have to agree.

4 August 1961

Three years since Nando's death. I thought the expression said having fun makes the time fly. It seems like yesterday since I stood at the grave, and it hasn't been three fun years. Yesterday was a terrible day for everyone. The three of us were stuck in the room all day with a bag of chips and one bottle of soda. I have never been so hungry in my entire life. On top of the food situation, the air conditioning was not working properly in our room. It had to be one of the hottest days of the summer. But, it seems like we had the best of it.

We haven't heard from Papi since he left two days ago with three other businessmen from Bayamo in a car. They were in a rush to get out of La Habana and make it back to Bayamo as soon as possible. They had heard rumors of an impending money exchange, and they needed to check on their businesses and get money as soon as possible. Papi left Mami with three thousand *pesos* and told her to get as much money as she could at the banks if, or when, the exchange happened. Mami left shortly after breakfast this morning and didn't return to the room till six in the evening.

We were ravenous, so Mami took us to Kimbo's Restaurant at the Hilton for dinner. She had a migraine and just wanted some fruit to eat. She asked the waiter for *fruta bomba*, which in Bayamo we call papaya. In La Habana, papaya is considered a derogatory slang word for a woman's nether regions. The waiter must have detected Mami's accent from Oriente, the easternmost province, because he yelled to the cook, "Cut up some papaya for the lady," with an emphasis on the word papaya. Mami was quiet throughout the entire dinner and was eager to get back to the hotel room.

When the check came Mami pulled out strange looking money and handed it to the waiter. J.J. noticed first and questioned Mami about the new currency. Mami held up a *peso* and said, "Che Guevara has issued new *pesos* for Cuba – see his likeness on the front. I stood in line all day to exchange my three thousand *pesos*. And, guess how many Che's I received in exchange? Two hundred *pesos* or *ches*! Tony, you're good with arithmetic. Does that sound fair to you?"

Mami was starting to make a scene in the restaurant, so I asked her to go to the bathroom with me. When we got in there, she started sobbing. I got her to calm down and told her we needed to get back to the hotel. Mami agreed with me. Tony wanted to ask questions as we walked back to the hotel, but Mami told us all she would answer our questions back at the room. This is Mami's story:

"After I left our room this morning I went down to the concierge's desk to get directions to the nearest bank so that I could exchange the money Papi had left me. A woman near me overheard my question and offered to take me because she was headed that way herself. Her name is María, and she is the kindest woman I have ever known in my entire 37 years. María led me to the nearest bank. You would not believe the size of the line leading out of the front doors. It must have been two blocks long!

"We stood outside in that line for hours and hours in the hot sun. You know how I get after being in the sun for thirty minutes. My head was pounding. María could tell I was in agony. People were sitting on their front stoops just watching us stand. María approached this older black gentleman and asked him for a glass of water for me. He immediately went inside his house and brought me back a *jarrito* (cup) with water. I asked if it would be alright if I sat down on his steps for a second, and he said of course.

"He wanted to know what was wrong, so I told him I get severe migraines, and I no longer had any aspirin. I had run out just the other day after Che announced Cuban women don't have aches and pains anymore. That man disappeared inside his house for a minute and returned with two aspirins! Then the nicest lady, probably the old man's wife, came out with a *café con leche* for me. I owe that family so much. I gave him one hundred *pesos*. If I had known at that point how little my money would be worth inside the bank, I would have given him so much more.

"María led me back to the line to wait some more. She held me up for a good twenty minutes before the aspirin and caffeine started to alleviate my headache somewhat. When we got to the door María told me to go first. I walked inside and found only one man sitting behind an enormous desk. On either side of him were some security guards with revolvers on their hips. I gave the man my remaining money, almost three thousand *pesos*, and he handed me two hundred *pesos* in exchange.

"I thought I would faint from the heat, the migraine and the enormity of what had just happened. I asked the man if I could sit down for a minute to compose myself. It was cooler and darker inside, just what I needed for my headache. He told me no, but one of the security guards said it would be okay, that he would keep an eye on me. María came in and got her two hundred *pesos* while I sat. Then, she helped me up and out of that bank."

Mami was exhausted from the day's events. I felt like a total piece of crap for having complained about eating potato chips and sitting in a warm room for the day. And, we were all worried about how Papi was faring in Bayamo. So, we called it an evening.

7 August 1961

Papi is back from Bayamo. And, we are now at the Hotel Lincoln. We were eager to leave the Hotel Bristol. The air conditioning in our other room never did work properly. And, we were excited to see our friends. Papi hasn't said too much yet about his short trip to Bayamo. He has called a family meeting for tonight after dinner.

I was looking forward to eating downstairs at our familiar restaurant with our favorite waiter, Eduardo. When we got to our table a new waiter we had never seen came over to take our order. His name is Jorge. He seems nice enough, but Mami thought something was off. According to Mami's hairdresser, also Eduardo's sister, Eduardo had been working at the Hotel Lincoln for five years. He is the one who found her a position in the hotel salon. Mami said she needed to get her hair done anyway, so she would inquire about Eduardo tomorrow.

8 August 1961

Our family meeting was depressing. Papi says he has been all but ruined by the currency exchange. According to Papi, Che Guevara and Fidel Castro have taken the final step toward making Cuba a communist nation. They have effectively leveled the economic playing field by stealing everyone's hard earned cash. The rich were now poor, and the poor were still poor.

Mami had worried needlessly for a couple of days thinking Papi would be mad that she only got two hundred *pesos* for her three thousand, but Papi explained it had been that way for every single person in Cuba. No matter how rich or poor the individual, Che had set the exchange limit for cash on hand to two hundred *pesos*. Mami could have walked into that bank with one million *pesos* and still only received two hundred in exchange.

In addition, no matter how much money you had saved in the banks only ten thousand of it was honored by the regime. So, Papi explained that, for instance, if you had a million *pesos* in the bank you were now worth ten thousand *pesos*. He wouldn't tell us how much he had lost, but the figure must have been devastating because Papi's voice was barely a whisper. Also, like every other Cuban still left on the island, he was only allowed to withdraw one thousand *pesos* from the bank. Each month starting in September he would be allowed to withdraw one hundred *pesos* from his personal funds. Poor Papi, poor us.

I asked Papi about the money he had hidden at home under the entrance foyer table. His eyes got huge. He asked, "You knew about that money?"

"Sure. Tony and I discovered your stash years ago when we were playing hide and seek. You must have had over ten thousand *pesos* in that envelope," I said.

"Probably more now. But, it doesn't matter. That money is worthless. We can burn it, use it to make paper airplanes or play our *Monopolio* (Monopoly) game. My emergency fund is worthless," he said.

"On the bright side, I've paid for the hotel through September. We don't owe any money on our houses or farms. And, I've already paid my contact in the communist government over ten thousand *pesos* to procure your exit visas," said Papi. "We should hear something in the next week or two about your tickets out of Cuba."

9 August 1961

Mami says Eduardo, our waiter, is now one of the many *desaparecidos* – the one's who have been "disappeared" by the government. Mami said she was at the salon getting her hair done by Rosa, his sister, when he asked about Eduardo. She told Rosa that the whole family missed him. Rosa gave her a tight smile. A few minutes later Rosa dropped her scissors and bent down to get them. While she knelt she whispered to Mami, "He has been gone for over two weeks. I visit the main prison, El Castillo del Principe, everyday. They won't tell me if they have him locked up. We don't know anything. We are out of our minds with worry."

All Mami could do was place a hand on Rosa's shoulder and squeeze. There are spies everywhere, even the salon, and we are watched. Mami said that on an earlier visit, Rosa had confided in Mami that the salon owner was a communist leader. Mami says we must be more careful than ever. We can't do anything to jeopardize our escape from Cuba.

10 August 1961

Castro gave an interview yesterday about the currency exchange. He talked for hours and hours on end. But, the gist of his message was that the currency exchange was absolutely necessary because so much of Cuba's money was abroad. The figure he quoted was twenty million *pesos* that had been taken or sent out of the country. Castro said he tried to stem the flow of money by annulling the five hundred bill, but that was a temporary and negligible step at best. Money kept being sent out of the country.

Castro also cited three other reasons for the exchange: (1) the Americans in Guantanamo were creating huge excesses in exchange for money to purchase goods in their black market, (2) CIA subterfuge and (3) Cubans hording money under mattresses instead of banks. For months Castro and Che had been preaching about the safety of the Cuban banking system, yet many Cubans were still afraid to save. The exchange would reward those individuals who had followed his advice.

Castro said that over four hundred million *pesos* went unexchanged by August 4th. That figure represented the amount of money that was held abroad or here in Cuba illegally. He justified his actions by saying that less than three hundred thousand people in Cuba were affected by his actions. These three hundred thousand people had saved more than ten thousand *pesos* in the bank. Those were the only people who held money legally and were hurt by his actions.

How does that thief talk to the Cuban people with a straight face? How does he sleep at night knowing what he has done? Why would he put such a corrupt individual as Che Guevara in charge of the banking system? Che is a murderer and thief masquerading as a revolutionary. How could Castro do this to the people he promised to end the corruption for? How?

13 August 1961

Tia Dolores arrived today with her three younger daughters.
Mami started the paperwork to get them out a while back, so
now they are going to stay at the Hotel Lincoln near us to
await their exit visas. Mami is happy to have her sister close
by again. Papi is glad too because he wants to return to
Bayamo, but he is reluctant to leave again so quickly. Tia
Dolores and her girls will keep us all occupied while he gets
back to the business.

We all had dinner together downstairs in the
restaurant. Tia Dolores was able to get a room near us, so
we are all fairly close together. It's nice to have some family
near us, although, we still have several friends awaiting their
chance to leave. Having a community makes this journey
more palatable. Whenever I start to think about moving to
the United States I get a bit panicky. I have to stay strong
because Mami and Papi look so fragile right now.

15 August 1961

Mami and Tia Dolores left today to visit the offices at Iberia
and check on the process of the visas. We all played
Monopolio, boys versus girls, in our suite to pass the time.
The game was still going on when Mami got back from her
errand. Everyone was bored with the game, so we counted
our stacks of money. The girls were winning before we
called it quits.

Mami said it shouldn't be much longer before
everything is finalized. She has an excellent feeling after her
visit today. Things have been progressing. If there was ever
any suspicion on the part of the soldiers that day in June,
nobody has bothered the secret offices in the Iberia Airlines
building. Mami is so relieved that Tia Dolores is with her.
They give each other strength and courage.

21 August 1961

Mami spoke with Papi yesterday. Papi is still stuck in Bayamo handling some business. He thinks it will be another week before he can join us again in La Habana. Mami is restless to see him, her parents and her home. She decided today that she is going to chance riding the Santiago-Habana Bus tomorrow. It's a twelve hour ride to Bayamo. She said it's very difficult and expensive to fly right now because of the currency exchange. Besides, she wants to surprise Papi.

Tony keeps begging Mami to go with her. Tia Dolores has volunteered to watch us all. In fact, since our suite is so much bigger, she's going to move in with us and save some money while Mami is gone. Tony is such a handful Mami is seriously considering taking him along for the ride. She thinks traveling with a younger child will help her odds of being left alone during the journey. They are both probably right, but I don't like being left behind.

25 August 1961

Mami and Tony are still not back from Bayamo. J.J. and I are bored. We spend our day playing cards, reading or watching the television. Tia Dolores doesn't want anything to happen to us on her watch, so she doesn't let us do anything on our own. We all have to go down to the restaurant together. I know she means well, but I feel like a prisoner. I can't wait for my family to get back. Doesn't she realize we are all going to be separated soon enough?

28 August 1961

Mami had quite a story for the rest of us when she got back yesterday. At least Papi is with us again. Mami said that she and Tony made the early bus leaving La Habana at eight in the morning. The bus was rickety and would stall out from time to time. It was having trouble keeping pace with the other cars out on the road. Plus, a soldier sat right in front of them for the entire journey. He was loud and overbearing and kept up a steady conversation with his comrade.

When they made it to Camaguey the bus driver announced he was stopping near a restaurant. There would be a considerable wait, so everyone was welcome to get off the bus and buy something to eat. The driver was hoping to switch buses because the current bus was in such a sorry state of disrepair. The restaurant only served small portions of rice and plantains, but at least it was some food. A man at the restaurant recognized Mami from the Hotel Lincoln and told her he and his wife would be happy to host them for the evening, but Mami was eager to get to Bayamo.

They probably waited three hours for the replacement bus. As they were getting back onto the bus, Mami thought the soldier was about to hit Tony in the head with his elbow. She yelled out before she realized who she was yelling at. The soldier turned around and told her to "control herself" and nothing would happen to the boy or her. Mami rode the rest of the way to Bayamo in a state of sheer panic.

They arrived at the bus depot in Bayamo a little after three in the morning. Mami was able to get a taxi to drop her off at the house. Tony and Mami were so excited to surprise Papi. They kept knocking at the front door for a couple of minutes without any response, so they worked their way back towards the master bedroom and tried to shake the iron scrollwork on the windows. Papi opened up the curtains and didn't recognize Mami at first. Then Tony yelled, "Papi let us in, it's us!"

Papi was really shocked when he opened up the door for them. In the poor evening light, Mami's hair looked blonde. She had let Rosa highlight it in La Habana when Tia Dolores arrived and had completely forgotten she looked different. Papi scooped them both up and gave them huge bear hugs and lots of kisses. They talked for a few minutes, but Tony and Mami were exhausted from the bus ride and collapsed in their beds.

Mami was so glad she had gone back to Bayamo because she got to see her parents again. She wants to send for them as soon as we get established in the United States. They will need someone to look after them soon, and Mami doesn't want to leave them behind.

Unfortunately, there was one bad incident while she was home. On the third day, there was some insistent knocking on the front door. As she approached the door she could see a soldier and a black girl standing on the stoop. Mami opened the door, and the soldier announced they were there to search the house. Mami said they looked under the furniture, moved the television, counted the glasses in the cupboards, rifled through music albums and even counted the number of dresses Mami had hanging in the armoire.

When Papi got home later that day, she told him what had happened. He said it has actually happened two other times while he's been at home. He didn't tell us because he didn't want any of us to worry. Mami is so angry. She has some really nice crystal, clothes and paintings that she won't need much longer. So, she organized all of her family to start dropping by periodically with things hidden in their bags that resemble our nice things. She's going to have them trade some of their cheaper everyday glasses, clothing and artwork for more expensive items. Why not?

Mami and Tony were hesitant to ride the bus back to La Habana, so Papi got tickets to ride the train again. Mami and Papi said the train was even fuller of Russians this time. You couldn't get a bite to eat or even anything to drink on the train. It was an uneventful but hungry and thirsty ride back. Mami did say a woman sitting near them gave Tony a sandwich from her purse. At least he didn't suffer too much.

1 September 1961
Mami and Papi placed a call to Tia Lola and Tia Caridad. They can't wait to meet us at the Miami airport as soon as we get the exit visas. They are living together for the time being to help each other with childcare and finances. Since there are already so many of them living under one roof, they are going to take me in and send me to a Catholic school in the neighborhood. I can take English there and finish my last year of high school. Tony and J.J. are going to live with Tia Virginia and Tio Enrique in Elizabeth, New Jersey. J.J. will attend the local high school, and Tony will start in junior high. I don't really understand all of these terms for the schools, but I am excited and frightened. I wish the three of us could stay together. But, it doesn't sound like anyone has room for all three. At least I will have some cousins, and Tony and J.J. will have each other.

7 September 1961
Today we celebrated what we hope will be my last birthday in Cuba. Mami took me to the salon first thing in the morning to get my haircut. I guess there's no use waiting to see Margarita again, so I let Rosa cut my hair. I asked her if she had heard anything about Eduardo, and she just shrugged her shoulders. I asked Mami for permission to get highlights, but she told me not to be ridiculous – that my hair is the color of coal and would look terrible any other way than natural. She is probably right. Mami's hair is

more cinnamon colored so the blonde blends in okay. I was just hoping for a different look to go along with a different home.

We didn't do much during the rest of the day until it was time for dinner. Mami and Papi managed to reserve a small room in the restaurant and had invited Tia Dolores and my cousins, the two remaining families from Bayamo, Doctor Alvarez and his wife and Rosa. We had a modest dinner and cake afterwards. Papi even managed to buy me a book, probably on the black market, of José Marti's poems for inspiration about what freedom means. I wonder if I will be allowed to take a book on the flight to Miami.

11 September 1961

A courier knocked at our door this morning a just after ten. Papi answered the door and was handed an envelope a little larger than letter size. He opened it up and looked at it for a moment and then asked everyone to gather around. It was the news we had been anxious to receive. Inside the envelope were three exit visas and three one way tickets to Miami, Florida.

We all looked at each other for a moment. Mami and Papi hugged each other, and then they turned towards us with tears in their eyes. We all came together crying, hugging and laughing. It was such a mix of emotions. I started crying hysterically and left the room and ran into the bathroom. I couldn't stop the sobbing and the tears. I was free. I was abandoned. I was excited. I was devastated. I hadn't known so many emotions could be felt at the same time.

12 September 1961

I couldn't write anymore last night. All of the same feelings surfaced, and I started my sobbing all over again. Sleeping helped some. And, I think I'm all cried out now. I just feel numb today. I feel like I'm just going through the motions – eating without tasting, dressing without paying attention to what clothes I select, smiling when my heart is breaking inside.

I realized after my emotional outburst yesterday that I never found out when we are scheduled to leave. Mami and Papi said we leave on September 22nd. I asked if we would go back to Bayamo one more time, but they both think there just isn't enough time to make the trip. The buses are unreliable, the train is crowded and it is almost impossible to get a flight these days. I can't believe I leave Cuba for good in ten days!

Mami and Papi promise they will join us as soon as they can. In fact, Papi has already arranged a false address for them since they are so well known in Bayamo. They are now citizens of Playa Santa Fé on the Isla de Juventud (Isle of Youth) for the exit visa process. Mami thinks it won't be too long before they can follow us over.

13 September 1961

Today we went to visit Mami's cousins in the wealthy section of La Habana, Miramar. We've dubbed them the DuBois sisters because they come from French aristocracy. It is poor form to show up at someone's house, especially the DuBois sisters' house, without a small gift. We walked toward Miramar so that Papi could buy them a small trinket or food item, but there's not much left in the city of La Habana. Papi eventually bought four plantains, a pitiful offering, but what could we do when the stores are empty?

As we walked, we were subjected to socialist propaganda belching from speaker placed high along the streets. The speakers would play excerpts from speeches that Castro or Che had given recently. Or, they would play

Mami's all time most hated song, the communist anthem called "The International." You could see the migraine just developing across her head whenever she heard that song. Luckily, we hailed a taxi because of the long distance from the hotel to Miramar and escaped the droning speakers for awhile.

The DuBois sisters were still reluctant to leave Cuba. They had their beautiful home in La Habana, and their connections were keeping them supplied with basic necessities. They thought they would weather out the storm as long as possible. Besides, they hated the United States on principle. Their father had died during the Spanish-American War of 1898 at the hands of an American soldier. And, they were not eager to leave Cuba for his murderer's land.

While we were visiting, the school across the street must have been having a concert or practice of some kind because we heard "The International" sung over and over. Mami was getting nauseous and asked Papi if we could leave. Mami told her cousins she wanted to get back to the hotel because her migraine was getting stronger. As we crossed in front of the school Mami started to sing the national anthem of Cuba, "La Bayamesa," and we all joined in. It was our small rebellion, but it gave us a little power and peace. Since it had been such a long walk to Miramar, we found a taxi as soon as we could.

When we got back to our suite Mami's youngest sister, Carmen was waiting in our room. What a surprise! Carmen is only 20 years old. Mami is going to help get Carmen out of Cuba too. Mami invited Carmen to stay with us. She plans to divide her time between Tia Dolores' room and our suite. Carmen is more like an older sister to me than a younger sister to Mami.

14 September 1961

Carmen joined us for breakfast this morning in the restaurant. We all ordered hot dogs, so she did too. When the waiter left she asked us why we were all eating hot dogs, and Papi told her there's not much else available these days. Even the hotels are starting to run out of food now. When the hot dog came Carmen said, "This smells awful. What is this?" The poor waiter stepped back and just stared at her. Mami told her that the hot dogs were imported from Russia in cans. Just about everything we were eating in the hotel was a canned good from Russia. It was food, awful food, but food nonetheless.

Papi invited Carmen to join us for the day. We were headed to Coney Island, a huge amusement park in La Habana. She was reluctant, but we dragged her along. It was a fun day. We rode just about every ride in the park. Carmen was scared to death of the roller coaster, but we got her on that too. I've never heard so much screaming in my life. When we got off the roller coaster Carmen's hair was a mess, and she was missing part of her heel of one of her shoes. We have no idea how that happened, but it was hilarious. Mami paid for a gypsy to tell our fortune. It was the same for all of us. We would be leaving Cuba soon. Papi said, "Any fool could have told you that."

15 September 1961

Papi had asked J.J. a few weeks back what he would like for his 19th birthday. We are scheduled to leave almost a month before he has his actual birthday, so Papi wants to celebrate in Cuba. J.J. wanted to eat at his favorite restaurant in La Habana, La Gallega (The Galician Girl). Papi did some checking and discovered that La Gallega had already been closed down by the government. He wasn't sure if it was because they had run out of food or because the owners were not communist sympathizers. J.J. wanted a seafood paella, so Papi promised to see what he could do.

In the middle of the afternoon Papi told us all to be ready at six in the evening. He told us to wear our finest clothes. At six sharp, Tia Carmen, Tia Dolores and the cousins and two families from Bayamo all came to our suite. Papi told J.J. tonight was his birthday celebration. When we got downstairs Papi had four taxi cabs waiting. We all piled in and rode out into the warm, dark night. I was sitting next to J.J. As we approached La Gallega his face lit up. We drove right past the restaurant, though, and he looked crestfallen. The taxis dropped us off in a small alley.

Papi led the way to a small, poorly lit door and knocked two times. The owner of La Gallega greeted us with a big smile. She put us in the back room, a windowless room, and served up the best paella I have ever eaten in my life. It was full of all of our favorite seafood – crab, oysters, clams, scallops, and even a little lobster. I felt a little guilty partaking of such a feast, but I reminded myself we had been eating smelly hot dogs at the hotel for weeks. On the ride home, J.J. kept thanking Papi for the extravagant gesture. Papi's response was, "It was the least I could do for my son. Yes, it was expensive, but you will take this memory with you when you leave Cuba. It was well worth the expense."

16 September 1961

We have some downtime today. Mami left with Carmen earlier to visit the Iberia office and get her exit visa process started. I had a chance to really spend some time reading José Marti's poems. I'm grateful that Papi found that book for me. One of his verses really struck a chord with me.

What matters that your dagger
Into my heart is plunged far?
I have my verses which are
More powerful than your dagger!

What matters that this great pain
Clouds the sky, and drains the sea?
My verse, sweet solace to me,
Is born with the wings of pain.

I wish I could express myself in that manner. Mami
has always loved poetry, both reading and writing. I don't
have her proclivity to create such beautiful stanzas. I
worked on some verse all day today, and this is the best I
could produce. It's a poem about truth, loss and suffering. I
call it "The Brier."

I
knew
the taste
the feel
the smell
of briers

I
felt them
prickle
dig
hurt
under my skin

I
held them
close

in my arms
and bled
to death

After rereading my poem, I realized I sound pretty depressed. Mami and Papi have been doing such a great job of keeping us busy and our minds off the fast approaching reality. But, today has been a time of quiet reflection. I can't believe we leave in less than one week.

17 September 1961

Mami and Papi planned another field trip for today. Carmen decided to stay in the hotel this morning, so it's just the immediate family. We went to Río Cristal, an incredible restaurant and water oasis. I had never seen anything like it. It must be the hugest pool in Cuba. There are three diving boards, one of which looks like it's three stories high. Tony and J.J. had brought bathing suits to swim a bit before lunch.

I was more interested in the music and lunch. There was supposed to be a female singer from Bayamo as the main entertainment. I was disappointed when our waiter told us she had been replaced by a "communist approved" singer from La Habana. She was pretty good, but, of course, she had to finish the set with "The International." Mami stood up when she heard the first chords and headed to the bathroom. I followed suit. I could hear Mami humming "The Bayamesa" softly. I think these small rebellions keep her sane.

Danger kept Tony sane. He was always pushing the limit with Mami and Papi. It was time for lunch, and Papi called out to Tony. Tony yelled back, "One more jump!" The pool was quite empty since the majority of the patrons were eating lunch. So, all eyes turned toward Tony. And, wouldn't you know it; he was halfway up the ladder for the highest diving board. Mami gasped when she saw what Tony intended. He walked right out to the edge, shook out his legs, lifted his arms high into the air and jumped. He tucked into the cannonball position and entered the pool with a huge splash.

When Tony emerged he had a huge grin on his face. Several of the patrons started clapping. He got out of the water, took a bow and headed towards our table for lunch. Mami and Papi had their stern faces on, but Tony won them over with his grin. The kid literally has no fear. He doesn't seem to be concerned about the fact that we are leaving Cuba in five days without Mami and Papi. I wish I was as nonchalant about the whole thing. I should just think of our upcoming exile as a grand adventure. Wishful thinking!

18 September 1961

Tony actually looked a little nervous this morning as we left the hotel for Doctor Alvarez's office. Today his braces will be removed because Mami and Papi don't know what to expect or do for an orthodontist in the United States. All of us went together. Papi had never been to his offices. He had always been busy with work before. Also, he is trying to spend as much time as he can with us these last few days. He doesn't want to speculate on how long it will take Mami and him to get their exit visas, but he hopes it only takes a couple of months.

Papi didn't want to show up empty handed at the doctor's office. Also, he felt like we owed him and his wife so much for helping us out with the exit visas. So, he left early this morning in search of a gift. He showed up two hours later. We were worried because we needed to leave within five minutes to make our appointment. Papi said the only thing he could find was an ugly olive green dress. The stores are completely wiped out, except for green clothing.

He asked Mami if green was the trendy color for the year, and she just laughed. Mami said it was either a Russian trend or a communist propaganda color or maybe both.

We didn't wait long to see Doctor Alvarez. In fact, the reception room was almost empty, which is pretty unusual. The receptionist ushered us all in to the office first. When the doctor came in Mami and Papi embraced him and thanked him. They explained the exit visas had come through and that we would be leaving within the week. Then, Papi handed him the unwrapped gift for Señora Alvarez. Papi apologized for not having a box or anything and explained the current state of inventory in the stores. Doctor Alvarez got tears in his eyes. Papi said, "It is just a token of appreciation. I wish I could have bought something for you too – a watch perhaps. You've done so much for our family."

Doctor Alvarez explained, "My wife was arrested on Saturday at our home. She was charged with political crimes against the state."

Mami gasped and said, "How can this be? Your wife mainly ushered patients in and helped the receptionist out with paperwork."

"I tried to keep her out of my dealings with the exit visa process. I was trying to protect her from exactly what happened. I knew the communists were watching me, especially recently. Soldiers would sit in the waiting room for hours at a time. Over a week ago my offices were searched, but they found nothing. I think they got anxious to find something, anything on me. They are probably questioning her as we speak to squeeze information out of her," he said. He started to choke up a bit.

Mami gave him a hug and said, "You need to be strong. Most likely she will be released soon."

"I hope so. I worry that when they figure out she doesn't know anything they might hurt her. God, I'm so frightened for her," said Doctor Alvarez.

Papi said, "Listen we can come back tomorrow if it's easier on you. In the meantime, I can check with my contact in the communist government to find out what he knows."

Doctor Alvarez replied, "No. Let's take care of Tony's braces right now. I'm sure he's eager to have them off. I would appreciate if you check with your contact. I have some other people checking as well. Maybe you will hear something while you are in La Habana."

"Of course. Anything we can do. Please let us know," said Papi.

Doctor Alvarez said, "Why don't you folks stay in here while I take care of Tony. We'll be done within the hour. I'll have the receptionist bring you some water and perhaps café. I wish I had more to offer you."

Mami was so impressed with him. She commented on how composed he remained through this ordeal. She thought Doctor Alvarez was a fine gentleman and person and was truly sorry for his wife. Papi gave Mami a big hug and said, "It could have easily been you. What if those soldiers in the jeep in front of Iberia had stopped you? What if you had been here when the offices were searched? What if one of your 'little rebellions' had set off a communist?"

Mami said, "Let's not think about all of this unpleasantness. We are here together. Our children, God willing, are leaving this island in four days. We have to focus on their freedom. We have to focus on getting ourselves out soon after they leave."

19 September 1961

Papi wants to show us La Habana from up high. He says the best place to see it the entire city is from the Habana Hilton, so he invited our entire group on the excursion. Tia Carmen is the only one who took him up on his offer. She's usually ready for any adventure. We headed over to the hotel after our canned hot dog lunch. *Para la porra*! Jeez! How do the Russians eat this stuff? Or, do they send us their crap?

Anyway, the hotel was magnificent. It's hard to believe Castro's soldiers haven't looted the Hilton yet. The casinos are closed. They were the pride and joy of Batista's regime. But, they have left the hotel untouched according to Papi. The doorknobs and fixtures are reported to be of solid gold. I don't know if it's true, but they looked like the real thing. The décor was plush. As we passed the pool I saw what must have been a showgirl dressed in a bathing suit covered in rhinestones or sequins.

We took the elevator up to the top floor – the viewing area. The windows were huge, floor to ceiling. Papi found two tables next to each other in the lounge and facing the windows. He ordered *mojitos* for everyone. We sat sipping our cocktails enjoying the view. You could see all of La Habana under us perched from our vantage point.

I wish we had gone to the hotel at sunset or early evening. I would have liked to see La Habana all lit up at night. I'm glad Papi brought us to the fanciest hotel in Cuba right before we leave for good. We have so many good memories from this week. They don't completely overshadow the bad, Doctor Alvarez's wife and our upcoming exile, but it has been a treat. Papi wants us to soak in the atmosphere of Cuba as best as we can to last a lifetime. I know I will be forever grateful to him.

20 September 1961

Two more days to go... I had to pinch myself when I woke up this morning. My life feels like a bad dream right now. Today is packing day. Doctor Alvarez was nice enough to give us some packing recommendations so that the process at the airport would be as painless as possible. He also gave Mami three suitcases for our trip. We are each allowed one bag. They are not really suitcases but more like duffel bags. The bags are called *gusanos* – the real reason behind the names of those who are fleeing Cuba – because they look like worms. Everything must fit inside the one bag. Each bag must weigh less than thirty four kilograms. I won't even be able to pick it up if it weighs that much. I weigh fifty kilograms soaking wet. With all of the restrictions Doctor Alvarez enumerated, my bag will probably only weigh five kilograms anyway! The rules are ridiculous.

Each person can bring one change of clothes, one set of undergarments and socks, one pillowcase, one lightweight blanket, one comb or brush, one toothpaste tube and toothbrush, one shampoo bottle, one deodorant can and one bar of soap. That is, of course, if you have any of those items. Basic necessities have disappeared from the store shelves. It's a wonder how some of the stores even stay open. The powers that be have been rationing items like toilet paper and toothpaste for months.

Now, the list of what is not allowed… We cannot bring an extra pair of shoes, no jewelry of any kind (including watches, wedding bands, earrings, rings, bracelets, cuff links, etc.), no perfume or cologne, no pictures, no books or journals and nothing else you want confiscated at the airport. Doctor Alvarez made it clear that the airport officials will confiscate anything that they damn well please. The officials especially like taking jewelry that they can resell on the black market. And, most importantly, absolutely no money or gold can be taken out of Cuba.

I only brought a fraction of the clothes I own to La Habana, but I still have a huge selection of dresses and outfits here. Most of my clothes were custom made, primarily at Tienda Gloria. I have some beautiful things made of the finest fabrics and laces with coordinating purses, shoes and accessories. I know I'm spoiled, but it's because Mami and Papi had modest upbringings. Mami's family was more established and her father owned a bakery. But, Papi's family came to Cuba from Spain with the clothes on their backs and not much else. Papi worked hard and long for his success, and he insisted that we always have the best.

I've been staring at the armoire for the better part of the day trying to select my boarding attire and my change of clothes for my new country. It sounds like a simple task, but I've been procrastinating and indecisive. Mami made my task even more difficult by informing me that women are allowed to carry a small purse. At least I can take some blush, lipstick and hand lotion with me. If they don't approve at the airport, I'll just leave my purse behind.

I finally settled on my two outfits before we went down to our smelly, canned hot dog dinner in the restaurant. On the airplane, I will wear a pale pink skirt and vest with a white blouse that was hand embroidered in pink, red, orange and yellow flowers. My extra dress is a plain blue dress that I can wear to school, church, lunch or dinner. It will give me the greatest flexibility because I don't know what my life and wardrobe will be like in the United States. It's so hard for me to imagine my new life. I will completely start my life anew in two days.

21 September 1961

We are all sad. None of us has the motivation to do or see anything today. We have wasted most of the day sitting and staring at each other. Papi told us he has paid off a communist official who works in the security area of the airport to oversee the three of us as we are searched and

processed. I asked what this mean. And, Papi replied,
"Normally your duffel bag is searched thoroughly and any
expensive or suspicious items are removed from the bag.
Then you are taken to a ladies or men's changing room and
asked to disrobe down to your undergarments. The security
personnel make sure that you are not smuggling anything
under your clothes or in your shoes."

I was shocked. I didn't realize the potential for a
strip search existed. Papi says it's usually not so vulgar, but
he wants to spare us any discomfort or embarrassment.
There have been cases of women smuggling diamonds and
gold in their heels or even undergarments. Papi wants me to
wear some flat shoes to discourage the security guards. He
also doesn't want us to take any risks. So, we are not
allowed to place any cologne, pictures, books or jewelry in
our bags – just in case the bags are thoroughly searched. I
asked Papi, "Can we at least bring one picture of the
family?"

Papi said, "I wouldn't take the chance. We will try
to get some pictures out when we come. Or, maybe we can
get family members to send us pictures in letters. We'll
figure something out. Don't worry."

"Papi what about my gold coin bracelet, heart ring
and Pantin watch that you gave me on my fifteenth
birthday? I don't want to leave those things behind. They
mean the world to me. Please?" I asked.

"*Mi hija*, there is no way you will be able to get the
ring or bracelet out of Cuba right now. They are obviously
expensive and attractive to security guards. As for the
watch, let's rough up the leather band a bit and smudge the
glass on the face. Pantin is not a well known brand. It's a
German watch, and maybe they won't be able to tell how
valuable it really is. If you decide to do this, you have to be

prepared to have it taken from you. I can't guarantee anything," said Papi.

"I want to at least try to get the watch out. Especially since you bought it from my best friend's jewelry store," I replied.

"Okay. You know, they were very smart. As soon as the Ordoños realized what was happening in this country, they packed up their jewelry and valuables on a yacht and left the island. I was too stubborn. I couldn't accept what Castro was doing for the longest time. And, even when I knew, I wasn't ready to leave. I wanted to stay and watch as he stole my *cafetal* and my equipment. Well, he's almost destroyed me. It shouldn't be too long now," said Papi.

All day long I worried about what would become of you, dear diary. First chance I had with Papi alone, I asked him if we could talk privately for a few minutes. "Of course, *mi vida* (my life). What's on your mind?" he asked.

I explained, "Will you hide this diary with the one I began a few years ago after Nando's death?"

"Of course," he replied.

"Without reading it," I countered.

"Yes. If that is what you want. I give you my word. I will not read your diary," he replied.

"Thank you Papi. Your word means everything to me," I said as I started to get tears in my eyes.

"Where exactly is your original diary hidden?" he asked.

"It is still under the loose panel at the bottom of my armoire, all the way to the right. Remember our little secret? I put the diary in a metal strongbox I found in your office. Mami told me I could have it," I replied.

Papi lifted an eyebrow and said, "Mami gave it to you?"

"Yes. I didn't take it. It was a smaller box that had a broken latch. Mami figured you were never going to use it. She saw me eyeing it one day and told me to get it out of the office before she threw it out. It must have been during one of her cleaning missions," I said.

"Well, are you ready to give me the diary now. Or, do you need to write something else?" he asked.

"I'll be ready in a few minutes. *Gracias*. Thank you," I said and gave him a hug and kiss. Papi held on extra long.

I have to say goodbye to you, dear diary. You've been a solace and friend these past three years. I will never be able to make sense of all of the things that have happened to me, my family, my friends and my nation at the hands of Castro. Tomorrow I will leave Cuba without my parents. There is no guarantee that I will ever see them again. Also, I've been told that I will be separated from Tony and J.J. in America. I can't even begin to fathom how hard the next twenty four hours will be.

Papi heard me sobbing and came back in. "What's wrong *mi amor* (my love)?" he asked.

"How will I have the strength to fly away from you, Mami and my nation tomorrow? How?" I asked.

Papi started to stroke my hair and said, "When my mother died a few years ago, I was devastated. You probably don't remember, or maybe I hid it well at home. One day I went to San Salvador and spoke with Father Francisco. He told me that I had to find some inner peace to get through the grief. He said when things got especially tough, there is a Jesuit prayer I could recite over and over until I felt better."

"Does it work Papi?" I asked.

"You'll have to see for yourself," he replied.

"Tomorrow as the plane is taking off I want you to say these

words to yourself. They may come in handy in the next few
months until we are reunited."

> Dear God, give me strength to bear my pain.
> Lord, Jesus Christ, please help it to go away.

"I will try to be strong for you and Mami
tomorrow," I replied. "I hope that this prayer really works."

Mami has barely spoken all day. I think she's afraid
to start crying in front of us. Poor Tony, he can feel the
tension in the air and has tried to entertain us with his crazy
antics from time to time. He came out earlier wearing one of
Mami's dresses, complete with hat and heels. At least
everyone laughed for a bit. And, J.J. has been as stoic as
ever. He will be our strong, silent rock in America.

Adios diary. *Adios* Cuba. *Adios* childhood. Dear
God, give me strength to bear my pain. Lord, Jesus Christ,
please help it to go away.

> Yours faithfully,
> *Daniela Isabela Badilla*

Closing Words

by Isabela Daniela de Leon

Upon my arrival in Cuba I was as enchanted as Christopher Columbus had been in 1492 when he declared, "This is the most beautiful land that human eyes have ever seen." I was so excited to visit my parent's homeland that I easily ignored the security guards in the airport that rifled through my backpack and luggage, counted my bracelets and rings and verified that I didn't have any recording devices of any kind on my person. I was glad they left my cheap camera alone. I wanted to take as many pictures as I could for my family.

If you could look past the posters of Castro, communist slogans and amplifier systems, Cuba must have looked almost identical to how my mother viewed it on September 22, 1961, when she had boarded her plane. Yes, the majority of the buildings desperately needed painting; they had been in disrepair for decades. The vintage cars were everywhere on the streets and in parking spaces. I looked for green Oldsmobiles like the one my grandfather might have driven. It's probably the romantic in me, but I was completely charmed by the island.

My cousin Manny had been to Cuba before to visit his family, and he easily negotiated tickets for us on the Santiago-Habana bus. It took us close to fifteen hours to make our way down to Bayamo. The bus was slow and even required a jump start at one of our stops. I wondered if anyone in my family had ridden the same bus before. When we arrived in Bayamo, Manny tried to hail a taxi, but they were few and far between. So, we walked about five kilometers to Tio Miguel's house. This was the house my grandfather had left in Miguel's care in 1961 when he left

Cuba for good. I couldn't wait to see where my mom had lived during her childhood.

Manny and I knocked for awhile before someone finally opened the front door. Manny hugged Tio Miguel and introduced him to me. He gave me a kiss on the cheek and commented on how much I looked like my mother. The sight of Tio Miguel took me aback. He was stooped over, not much taller than me, thinning white hair and had eyes glazed over with cataracts. What shocked me the most, however, was how thin and frail he looked. I had always been thin like my mother. But, when I looked at Tio Miguel, I thought he must weigh less than me.

He invited us in. Again, I felt like when I first arrived in Cuba. I don't think much had changed since my mother's family had left the house. Everything was neat and tidy. But, there were obvious signs of use. The seat cushions were sagging. Wood pieces had nicks and scratches. The entire house needed painting. Overall, the house looked sad and tired, just like Tio Miguel.

His wife had passed away years ago, and my mother's older sister, Eva had moved in to help out. She came in from the patio and greeted us warmly. She too was stooped, frail and thin. Her face reminded me of my grandmother, and she saw my grandmother and mother in my face. She took me to my mother's old room and told me I would be staying here. I was elated, not only because it was my mother's old room but because I would have a chance to search for her diary.

I hadn't realized how tired and hungry I was until I sat down on my mother's bed. I took some time to soak in her room. She had cream colored walls, the same ivory marble tile that ran throughout the rest of the house I had seen and painted furniture in a very pale shade of pink. Her bedspread was off white with pink flowers embroidered all over the top and sides. There was also a huge armoire that ran the length of one wall, also painted in a pale shade of pink. This room didn't appear as worn and tired as the living and dining areas I had seen already. But, I must have really been tired because I dozed off fully dressed on top of the bedspread.

When I woke up by my watch I had taken a three hour nap. Someone had come in and removed my shoes and covered me with a light blanket. I could hear voices and I followed the sounds to the dining room. Tio Miguel, Tia Eva and Manny were eating some rice and beans. I joined them at the table and ate what was offered. It wasn't much food, but it was enough to kill the hunger pains in my stomach. Manny had already briefed me on the bus ride down. There would be little food while we were staying with family. There is a quota system for basic staples such as rice and beans, and each family gets one small chicken per month. The last time he had visited, the family had insisted that he eat the biggest part of the chicken which was tiny by our standards in America.

Two of my ten days of vacation were already gone, and I was eager to see more of the island. We would only have five days in Bayamo because Manny wanted to give us plenty of time to get back to Havana for our flight home. He was also worried about burdening the family for food. He said that anyone we would visit during the trip would insist on feeding us from their meager food pantries. It would be rude on our part to refuse to eat, so he wanted to spread our dinners between different locations. He explained there is hardly anything available for purchase, even on the black market.

Also, we had both brought extra socks, undershirts and underwear to distribute among the family. We would then pack their old items in our luggage so that the security

guards in the airport wouldn't notice any items missing. I
brought along four pairs of shoes plus the ones I was
wearing on the flight. I was hoping at least one or two
people would benefit from a shoe swap. My grandmother
had told me it is almost impossible to purchase shoes in
Cuba these days.

Ever since the collapse of the Soviet Union, the
Cuban population has suffered greatly. Without their
biggest aid and trading source, the Cuban economy is on the
verge of collapse. It is difficult to purchase gasoline for cars.
The electricity service is sporadic. In some areas it only
comes on for one or two hours a day – right before dinner
for cooking purposes. Clean drinking water is scarce. It's
not uncommon to see most people on foot, bicycle or even
oxen and horse. There is a small economic resurgence in the
travel industry. Castro has opened hotel ownership
possibilities to Europeans and Canadians. But, Havana is
the main beneficiary. The rural areas are dirt poor.

We talked for awhile after dinner with Tio Miguel
and Tia Eva. Manny and I were both tired, so we headed off
to our rooms early. I was eager to start searching for my
mother's diaries. When I opened the armoire doors I found
an empty expanse. Tia Eva had already told me at dinner
that through the years she had given away my mother's
clothes to family members and friends that could wear her
size. I felt the bottom of the armoire from left to right and
could not find any apparent weaknesses or areas where the
paneling gave a bit. I didn't want to damage my mother's
furniture, but I was desperate to search further. I took off
my shoes thinking my entire body weight might loosen the
paneling. Again, I tested the floor from left to right. Still
nothing.

I didn't want to get Manny involved, but I needed
help. I found him still awake in what would have been one

of my uncle's rooms. He came back to my room and checked out the armoire. Then, he looked at me and said, "For a college graduate you sure don't have a lot of common sense. Go see if you can find a knife in the kitchen." I came right back with a knife, and he used it to feel around the base of the armoire to see if he could wedge it between the frame and the panel itself. Within a minute he found a spot where the knife slid in easily. Sure enough, a long piece, probably three feet long, lifted right up. Manny was right. I would have kept on pushing on the wood instead of trying to lift it up.

Right in the corner was a small, metal strongbox. I pulled it slowly out. There was a lot of rust on the metal, probably from years of sitting in such a humid climate. Manny offered to leave so that I could have some privacy when I opened my mother's box. I was actually a bit nervous and afraid and asked him to stay. My hands were shaking so hard I could hardly lift the lid. I took a deep breath and opened the box.

I was expecting to only see two notebooks inside the box, and they were there. But, on top of the notebooks was a twice folded piece of paper. It was not lying flat, and you could definitely see something was inside. When I lifted up the paper it felt heavy. As I opened it, a ring and bracelet fell into my lap. The bracelet was a thick chain rope of eighteen carat gold with a huge coin charm. The ring was also of eighteen carat gold. The top of the ring was shaped like a heart, and there was a single large pearl nestled in the heart. My mother had spoken of this jewelry before. I think it's what my grandparents gave her on her fifteenth birthday. The note read:

1 October 1961

Dearest Daughter,

I miss you more than words can say. I am a broken man. A man is nothing without his children, and I have sent mine away. I hope that my decision was correct.

I wanted to die in the airport as I watched your plane taxi away. Did you see me? I was the tallest man at the window with tears streaming down my face. I don't even remember how your mother got me back to the hotel.

We left La Habana immediately. I had to get back to my home. But, instead, an empty house greeted me. The silence was deafening.

Do you remember the prayer I taught you on your last day in Cuba? It worked when my mother passed away, but it is not working anymore. With each day that passes, I miss my children more and more.

I hope that you all are safe and sound in America. I wait for the day that your mother and I can join you. If it's not soon, I will go out of my mind. I have made bargains with God. I have pleaded to God. I must have my children.

Here is the ring and bracelet you wanted to take out of Cuba. I hope that you can one day wear this jewelry again. I love you with all of my heart.

Besos (kisses),
Papi

Manny and I were both crying when we finished reading the note. I vowed to Manny that I would somehow get the note and the jewelry to my mother. These items belonged with her, no matter the cost. Manny agreed that I should try to smuggle them out. He announced he was going to visit his grandmother tomorrow. I told him that I would like to stay here and read my mother's notebooks while he's gone. Before he left, we got the paneling back in place.

I spent the entire day reading my mother's diary. Her stories made me cry, laugh, long for another place and time and cry again. She had a remarkable childhood and upbringing in Cuba. It made me appreciate her more. It made me regret some of the things I had said and done through the years. Most of all, it made me appreciate my freedom all the more. I really shouldn't have made the journey while her childhood monster was still alive, but I'm glad I did, just the same.

I had a lovely visit with my relatives. I got to meet some of the family that I had heard discussed through the years. They all agreed that I had to get my mother's belongings back to her. Between Manny and Tio Miguel, they devised a plan. Luckily, I had worn three bracelets on my right wrist and multiple rings. Unfortunately, everything was silver. If the security guards made a note of that, I would be detained.

Using toothpaste, pulverized coffee grounds and ashes from the stove, my uncle and cousin created a paste that temporarily dyed my mother's gold jewelry a grayish silver hue. To further disguise the coin on the bracelet, I took a cheap metal decoration that hung from my backpack and pried it apart into halves. We placed a dot of glue on each side of the coin and covered it with my backpack charm hoping they would be easily removable once out of the country.

Manny and I had an uneventful trip back to Havana and made it back for our flight with plenty of time to spare and sightsee. After reading my mother's diary, some of the appeal and romance of Havana had worn off. The soldiers dressed in their olive drab attire stood out. Castro's face on billboards and signs physically sickened me. And, the appalling neglect of the buildings and abject poverty of the population made me so sad. I was glad to leave Cuba and didn't encounter any problems with security before I boarded the flight.

I successfully smuggled into Cuba some desperately needed items for my family and smuggled out my mother's diary and beloved jewelry. I longed to see my parents and give my mother her long hidden but not forgotten items. But, more importantly, I longed to tell her, "I understand. Now, I understand."

Epilogue

Daniela Isabela Badilla was reunited with her parents on January 1, 1962, after a three month separation. The Badilla family settled in Elizabeth, New Jersey. They temporarily lived with some family members. At the age of 43, the once successful and wealthy coffee grower, supplier and multiple café owner, my grandfather, found work as a fork lift operator making $1.17 per hour. He refused three separate offers to restart coffee businesses in America, Puerto Rico and the Dominican Republic. Within two and a half years he purchased a three story home in America. The three children eventually married. My mother, Daniela, was reacquainted with Julian de Leon at a mutual friend's home in New Jersey. Julian was lucky enough to leave Cuba on July 12, 1962, as part of the Peter Pan Flight that airlifted 14,000 minors from Havana to Miami. Daniela and Julian had two daughters.

The End

Acknowledgements

This novel would not have been possible without all of the stories my grandmother, Buela, told me through the years. While I was writing she would eagerly answer my questions and field my many phone calls at all hours of the day and night. When I was stuck or frustrated, Buela would tell me another story or memory from Cuba. *Gracias*, Buela. I especially like her ending for each story, "*Todo eso lo pasamos nosotros*." She would shake her head in disbelief trying to come to terms with what had happened to her family at the hands of *El Monstruo*.

Thanks dad. The computer chip in your brain enriched the historical accurateness of the novel. Your comments and edits kept the novel on track. And, your idea for the cover art was excellent. Mom, thanks for lending me your voice – your love of Cuba and your pain at its hands.

None of this would have happened without the National Novel Writer's Month contest. This story has been percolating inside of me for decades. Thanks for the push! I had two false starts, a paragraph long each, through the years. I'm forever grateful I stumbled upon www.nanowrimo.org. You guys are right; November is the perfect month for writing. I still can't believe I wrote this novel in thirty days.

Evan, thank you for beginning this journey with me, as part of the Young Writer's Program. I hope you finish your novel too. Dale, thanks for not complaining too loudly about picking up the slack as I wrote each afternoon and night.

And, last but not least, thanks to all of my family, friends, clients, fellow readers and the Lofthouse Book Club. Every one of you kept me accountable and motivated.

Printed in the United States
212750BV00004B/9/A

9 780979 487705